The Beauty of Bath Intrigue

The elegant resort town of Bath adored gossip—
and loved scandal even more. No wonder, then,
that Miss Perdita Grant was so very talked-about.

First, of course, there was her fortune—a fortune
that her handsome, dissipated, and deeply-in-debt
cousin Bertram Tillot would stop at nothing to
possess.

Then there was her beauty that surely could not
be ignored by the Duke of Anderly on her
frequent visits to his bedside, since that notorious
nobleman never had been known to leave a fair
flower unplucked.

Finally, there was the fierce feud between her
and the duke's hellion son, Lord St. Ive ...
and the fond attentions of the good Mr. Gilles,
who generously offered to give her his name to
save her reputation.

What would become of Miss Perdita Grant?
Society waited with baited breath and barbed
tongue for the answer—and Perdita herself
desperately wished she knew. . . .

Bath Intrigue

Bath
Intrigue

by

Sheila Walsh

A SIGNET BOOK

NEW AMERICAN LIBRARY

NAL BOOKS ARE AVAILABLE AT QUANTITY DISCOUNTS WHEN USED
TO PROMOTE PRODUCTS OR SERVICES. FOR INFORMATION PLEASE
WRITE TO PREMIUM MARKETING DIVISION, NEW AMERICAN LIBRARY,
1633 BROADWAY, NEW YORK, NEW YORK 10019.

SIGNET TRADEMARK REG. U.S. PAT. OFF. AND FOREIGN COUNTRIES
REGISTERED TRADEMARK—MARCA REGISTRADA
HECHO EN CHICAGO, U.S.A.

SIGNET, SIGNET CLASSIC, MENTOR, PLUME, MERIDIAN
and NAL BOOKS are published by New American Library,
1633 Broadway, New York, New York 10019

First Printing, May, 1986

1 2 3 4 5 6 7 8 9

PRINTED IN THE UNITED STATES OF AMERICA

Chapter 1

"CURSE THIS FOR a one-sided game!"
   The vehement cry pierced the hushed air of the crowded room with awesome clarity, sending little eddies of shock through the more dedicated of its present incumbents, annoying the rest, and generally threatening the atmosphere of discreet opulence so carefully contrived by the owner of this, London's newest, most fashionable gaming hell.

The perpetrator of the outrage, a veritable tulip of fashion, occupied a place at the table nearest the door. His fleshy, too-handsome features bore the evidence of prolonged overindulgence—evidence that a near-empty bottle set within hand's reach seemed all too clearly to confirm. It was not the first time his voice had been heard arguing about the run of the cards, and tempers were becoming frayed.

"Devil rot you, Tillot! If the pace is too hot for you, stand down, man!"

This suggestion inspired others around the table to join in, agreement vying with more sanguine advice until finally, with a muttered curse, the offender pushed back his chair and rushed from the room.

There was a palpable silence during which the Marquis of St. Ive lowered his quizzing glass with a faint sigh, leaned back in his seat, and crossed one elegantly pantalooned leg over the other. One straying quiff of fashionable swirling dark hair adorned his brow, lending him a particularly raffish look as he contemplated his friend through half-shut eyes.

"My dear Freddie," he murmured, more in sorrow than in anger, "I feel I must protest. When you persuaded me that this place was all the crack, you omitted to mention that it was also a venue for every kind of riff and raff who might seek admittance."

The Honorable Frederick Ponsford cocked a wry eyebrow, but declined to take issue.

"Oh, I say, that's coming it a bit strong, St. Ive!" Sir Geoffrey Blunt protested good-naturedly from across the table. "Don't say much for the rest of us, what?"

The gentleman sitting beside Sir Geoffrey tittered audibly, and found himself the recipient of one of St. Ive's most quelling stares, an awesome experience for anyone. He shifted uneasily and fell silent.

Freddie Ponsford viewed the incident with some misgivings. Devil take Ivo! That vivid face of his, overlaid as ever with boredom, could be damnably off-putting. It was the nose, of course—a magnificent but daunting appendage that even in Ivo's more amiable moments had been known to unnerve strangers. Freddie ventured a placating observation about "the occasional rotten apple."

A momentary gleam lit the marquis's eyes. "Precisely, dear boy. And we all know what that can do to a barrel of wholesome fruit."

In the face of such implacable reasoning, Freddie subsided with a wry grin.

Not so the tittering gentleman, Newns by name. Encouraged by his lordship's unexpected touch of whimsicality, he rallied, his bruised ego instantly restored. "Quite so, my lord," he said unctuously. "Though in this instance one cannot but feel for the poor unfortunate fellow. Mr. Tillot, for that is his name, has been cruelly used by fate."

"Indeed?"

Freddie recognized the danger in that single drawled utterance and held his breath. Surely even an egregious oaf like Newns must hear it too and acknowledge the folly of proceeding? But Sir Geoffrey's guest seemed determined to rush blindly to his doom.

"Yes, indeed. The young gentleman was so obliging as to honor me with his confidence earlier this evening, perhaps recognizing in me a sympathetic spirit, though I fear that even then he was in his cups, and not without cause. He had, it seems, an aged relative—an uncle on his mother's side of the family. . . ." In his eagerness to impart the full drama of the story, Mr. Newns was impervious to the growing mood of restless irritation among his companions, who were heard to mutter that they hadn't come to Quincy's to listen to some windbag boring on about this Tillot fellow's sojourn in Bath, where he had attended the funeral of the said aged relative.

"Would that they had buried his nevvy with him," some wit was heard to remark, but Mr. Newns, though he flushed, was now well embarked upon his peroration and refused to be discouraged.

"There being little in the way of dependents," he continued, "Mr. Tillot not unnaturally cherished expectations. . . . I gather that his financial affairs are in somewhat desperate straits, and clearly he hoped to be much plumper in the pocket as a result of his uncle's demise. But alas, it is not to be. . . ." He glanced around the table as though hopeful that his audience would by now be hanging on his every word, and was disconcerted to find them instead registering degrees of disinterest, while the marquis appeared to have fallen asleep, his chin sunk deep in the intricate folds of his cravat. Newns's ebullience at last began to waver, and he brought his story to a swift conclusion.

"Mr. Tillot was mortified to discover that he has been entirely cut out of this will by some chit of a granddaughter who has inherited the whole of a not inconsiderable fortune. And furthermore, his lawyer seems to hold out little hope that the will can be overset."

Into the ensuing silence came an inebriated voice, suggesting with facetious finality, "Well, the answer's as plain as your nose. Let him marry the wench."

It was not the response that Mr. Newns had hoped for, and in consequence his reply was a shade peevish.

"You may be sure that he had already tried his luck with the young lady while her grandparent still lived, only to be spurned for his pains." He tittered again, but nervously now. "He gained the impression both then and later, during the reading of the will, that her ambitions lay quite elsewhere . . . in short, in hope of becoming a duchess!" He brought the word out with an air of triumph, convinced that this must gain the attention of his audience where all else had failed. "There is an ailing and decidedly elderly nobleman who has considerable estates on the outskirts of Bath—"

St. Ive's chair, which had begun to rock ominously back and forth, came to rest with a resounding thud. "At last you begin to interest me, sir. A duke, you say?"

Freddie Ponsford's attention had long since wandered. He was brought back to a state of awareness by a curious inflection in his friend's voice. His wavering concentration groped for and fixed upon the nub of Newns's tedious peroration. He sat up.

"I say, Ivo—did the fellow say Bath? That's where your—"

"Be silent, Freddie." The marquis raised an admonishing hand. "I believe Mr. Newns is about to enlighten us further."

His glance strayed back to the unfortunate gentleman, who was by now in receipt of an urgently whispered communication from Sir Geoffrey, and was fast turning an unbecoming shade of puce beneath the intensity of his lordship's regard.

"Well, sir?" St. Ive intoned silkily. And as the other's mouth opened and closed without a sound: "Come now—you really cannot deprive us of the *pièce de résistance*. Your informant was so very forthcoming in every other respect—I feel sure he must have divulged the name of this so fortunate nobleman?"

Chapter 2

*T*HE MORNING WAS SHOWING early promise. A shaft of sunlight had already penetrated the breakfast parlor at Marston Grange to flirt among the crockery, giving added brightness to a cheerful jug of marigolds in the center of the table, and silvering the neatly coiled fair hair of the younger of the two ladies seated there.

Miss Perdita Grant was grateful for its small thread of warmth as she set down her teacup and opened yet another letter of condolence.

A moment later her companion was roused from abstraction by something sounding remarkably like a chuckle. Persuaded that she must have been mistaken, Miss Midgely addressed her former pupil in tones of gentle inquiry. "Did you say something, dear? Forgive me, I was not attending."

The eyes that lifted to meet hers were large and quite out of the commonplace, being of a clear light gray, darkly ringed and thickly fringed with fair curling lashes—eyes that could, on occasion, be disconcertingly direct; at present—yes, at present they did indeed hold a distinct twinkle.

"Wicked of me, I know, but quite irresistible in the circumstances." The page fluttered in her hand.

"From Miss Prothero. . . She is, so she informs me, prostrated with grief at Grandpa's passing, and I couldn't help but picture his face, were he but privileged to have known of it! Can you not imagine what he would say?"

There was a small silence, broken by Miss Midgely, her voice a prim echo of the schoolroom. "No, dear, I cannot. Nor should I dream of attempting to do so. It would be indelicate in the extreme for either of us to speculate upon such matters." She then confounded this fine reasoning by doing just that, avowing that Sir Edwin for all his quirks had been a gentleman to his fingertips, and could, she was sure, have been relied upon to say and do everything that was proper. This brought fresh mirth.

"Oh, what a hum, Midge, when you know as well as I that he took Euphemia Prothero in the strongest aversion from their very first meeting— and she disliked him with equal cordiality! Why, they never met once, to my knowledge, but they fell to brangling!"

The silence this time was more marked. Perdita regarded her dear friend and onetime governess with a rueful grimace.

"I'm sorry. I fear I have shocked you."

"Certainly not. I hope I know better after all these years than to mistake levity for light-mindedness." The older woman stifled a sigh. "To be sure, I still account it one of my few failures that I never managed to cure you of your tendency to at times treat serious matters with a disturbing want of gravity, though I have long since come to the conclusion that you most often do so out of a desire to conceal your true feelings."

There was so much true regard and sensibility in this practical observation that Perdita felt a stupid pricking behind her eyes. She blinked and at once sought refuge in flippancy. "What a charitable woman you are, Midge. I really don't deserve you." The words rang false even in her own ears, but she ignored the reproving "tut-tuts" and gave her attention once more to the waiting pile of correspondence, only to find the conventionally worded messages of condolence impossible to take in. She lifted her eyes to stare a little blindly out of the window.

Midge is right, of course, she mused pensively. Because it isn't that I don't care. In fact, I miss Grandpa quite wretchedly—more than I would have thought possible. If I find it so incredibly difficult to admit my sense of loss even to myself, then the fault must lie as much with him as with me. "Mark me well, child. I don't want to see tears, and I can't be doing with womanish megrims! Remember that, and we shall deal tolerably well together!" She could hear his voice clearly, even after twenty years, so clearly that he might well have been in the room. It had been a difficult ultimatum for a four-year-old child to grasp, and had her nature been less amenable, her life might have had a very different outcome.

"Beg pardon, ma'am." A voice came tremblingly to break in on her thoughts.

It was the new little maidservant hovering at her shoulder, chewing her lip apprehensively as she waited.

"Mr. Fletcher said I was to ask if there is anything more you'll be wanting."

Perdita pulled herself together and smiled. "I think not." She glanced at her companion, who shook her head. "No, thank you, Molly. We shall do very well as we are."

"Such timidity," said Miss Midgely as the door

was carefully closed. "You would never credit that that girl came from a family of seven children!"

"I daresay the change in her situation might well serve to make matters worse. Her life here must seem very different." Perdita picked up another letter and broke the seal. As her eyes scanned the page, she exclaimed, "Oh no! Really, how very petty!" And, reading swiftly to the end, "But how very like him! You will not be astonished to learn, Midge dear, that Cousin Bertram holds me entirely responsible for the terms and general tone of Grandpa's absurd will! He further advises me that he consulted lawyers the moment he returned to London—presumably with a view to having the will overset."

"Much good that may do him," declared Miss Midgely with the light of battle in her eyes. "You may depend upon it—Sir Edwin will have taken all the necessary steps to ensure that he can do nothing of the kind."

"Yes indeed. Mr. Barton assured me of that when Bertram swept out in such high dudgeon." Perdita sighed. "Though I cannot but wish that Grandpa had been a little kinder to him, or that he had at least couched his opinions in less trenchant language!"

The scene in the library was still vivid in her mind—tooled leather and heavy oak paneling, the rain rattling against the windows and the faint aroma of cigar smoke, so painfully evocative of her grandfather, still lingering on the air. The small party gathered there had done little to dispel the atmosphere of gloom. Mr. Windlesham cleared his throat a great deal, though whether out of necessity, or—as seemed more likely in retrospect—in nervous expectation of the trouble that lay ahead was not clear at the time. Certainly the mantle of

executor, which he shared with Mr. Barton, lay
heavily upon him as he studiously avoided Sir Edwin's wing-backed chair and frowned when Bertram swaggered across and made himself odiously
at home in it.

Perdita had been no more than mildly interested
as the lawyer's sonorous voice intoned a list of
minor bequests. These completed, Mr. Barton
paused, and there was something about that pause
which seemed to command her attention.

"And to my nephew, Bertram Tillot," he resumed
with rather more precision, "I leave my good wishes
for his future, in the firm belief that he has enjoyed
as much financial support from me during my
lifetime as any man has a right to expect. . . ."

Poor Bertram! His rage at this insult was scarcely
assuaged by Sir Edwin's final pronouncement. "The
residue of my estate I leave to my granddaughter,
Perdita Maria Grant, unconditionally, in the certain knowledge that the sound common sense with
which she has been blessed will prove an adequate
safeguard against rogues, charlatans, and importu-
nate suitors. . . ."

Perdita preferred not to recollect the uproar that
had followed. She might have felt more sorry for
Bertram had he shown the least hint of restraint,
but he had always been a poor loser, even as a
youth. She folded the letter and laid it aside.

"I thought I might drive into Bath this morning," Miss Midgely was saying. "My library books
must be returned, and that new haberdasher in
Milsom Street promised faithfully that the black
bombazine that I ordered would be in by today."
She paused. "I suppose you would not care to
come with me? A little fresh air would do you no
harm."

Perdita imagined the many people, good-intentioned for the most part but curious withall, who would wish to commiserate with her. She must face them eventually, of course, but not quite yet.

"I think not," she said with an offhandedness that did not fool Miss Midgely for one moment. "There are so many tedious chores still to be accomplished, and I really must settle down to answer some of these letters. I had no idea so many people held Grandpa in esteem."

"And so they should. Sir Edwin never made a show of doing good, but there are plenty hereabouts with cause to be grateful to him."

Miss Midgely looked keenly at Perdita. The severity of the simple mourning dress made her skin seem almost transparent and emphasized the weary smudges beneath her eyes that bore mute evidence to the many nights spent at Sir Edwin's bedside. And although it was not in Perdita's nature to be down-pin for long, the disgraceful behavior of Bertram Tillot, coming as it had on top of everything else, had indisputably left its mark.

"You know, my dear," she said, "you are quite right about there being a lot to do. It won't signify in the least if I postpone my visit to Bath until another day."

But Perdita would have none of it. "Good heavens, Midge! I shall hardly fall into a green-and-yellow melancholy if I am left to my own devices for a few hours. Besides which," she added with disarming candor, "if I should feel disposed to succumb to a bout of self-pity, I had far rather do so alone."

Miss Midgely's grunt covered a multitude of emotions, but she stood up with an air of briskness as if to acknowledge that further argument would prove useless. When she had gone, however, Perdita found great difficulty in settling to anything. She had expected to feel a sense of loss; her grandfather had been a big man in so many ways that his going must inevitably leave a vacuum in her own life. What she had not bargained for, and therefore found disconcertingly poignant, was the degree to which his presence still permeated every corner of the house—and nowhere more so than in the small study-cum-parlor close by the front door where he conducted his business affairs. She had been inside only once since his death, and that to admit Mr. Barton, relieved that she could leave him to deal with all the clutter of papers. Now she had to nerve herself to enter, to sit at Grandpa's desk and pick up his pen.

Her first shock was to find everywhere as neat as a new pin—the only occasion she could recall having seen it so. It seemed so alien to his character that she felt outraged on his behalf—and bereft. For the first time she experienced to the full the emptiness of his going—and for the first time the tears came, hard tearing sobs that left her weak and shaken. He had been father, mother, confidant, and friend, but he had also taught her to face life squarely, so after a few moments she wiped her eyes, gave a couple of defiant sniffs, and applied herself resolutely to the task of mending his pen so that she could make a start on the letters.

For a while she worked diligently, but then her concentration began to waver and her eyes were drawn to the window and beyond, where the sunlight touched the new green of the trees and dappled the long curving approach to the house. Marston Grange was a gracious well-proportioned building, Palladian in style and set on high ground, its front lawns falling away dramatically to afford its occupants what was widely acknowledged to be a rare panoramic view of distant Bath. A gap in the trees at one point disclosed the traffic passing to and fro along the Bath Road, and as Perdita looked she saw the Windlesham barouche-landau, quite unmistakable, with the rotund figure of Mrs. Windlesham sitting bolt upright among the cushions. It vanished from view and appeared a few moments later winding its way sedately around the long sweep of the drive to disgorge that lady, ostentatiously arrayed in her blacks, at the front steps. Perdita sighed and rose with mixed feelings to go and meet her.

"At last I am able to come to you, my dear," Mrs. Windlesham exclaimed, puffing mightily from the exertion of climbing the short pair of stairs to the drawing room. "Only fancy my poor Clarissa succumbing to the measles so close to her sixteenth birthday! Mr. Windlesham will have told you all about it, no doubt . . . how the child would not be left for a moment. . . ."

"Yes indeed." Perdita remembered the lawyer's dry-as-dust account and added gravely, "Such a distressing thing for you all. I do hope Clarissa is now much improved?"

"Dr. Bryant assures us that the worst is over, though she is as weak as a newborn kitten, of course. Still, that will pass, and with the summer just around the corner, we may hope for a steady improvement. But it grieved me nonetheless not to have been with you. . . . I charged Mr. Windlesham with all kinds of messages for you."

Perdita assured her that her husband had said everything that was proper in the circumstances.

"Well, so I should hope. But we know, do we not, that gentlemen do not always see things as *we* see them. It was his opinion that you would not be wishing to entertain callers at the present, but I

hope that we have been friends for too long to be
standing upon such terms!"

"Indeed, ma'am, you are most welcome," said
Perdita, hiding a smile. "A poor thing it would be if
I were not at home to my friends."

"Exactly so, my love—and so I told Windlesham.
Perdita ain't one to turn mopish for all that she has
sustained such a grievous loss!"

She settled herself comfortably in her favorite
chair and accepted with alacrity the offer of refreshment upon learning that her young friend
had been about to take a cup of chocolate.

"Such a pleasant sunny room," she prattled on
as Perdita rang for Fletcher and requested him
with a speaking look to put two cups on the tray
with her chocolate and perhaps a few of cook's
special shortbread biscuits.

Fletcher murmured that he would inquire about
the biscuits, his lugubrious features not betraying
by so much as a flicker that he knew chocolate to
be his mistress's least favorite beverage. As he
closed the door Perdita came and took her place
opposite Mrs. Windlesham.

"I confess that this is the room in the house that
I love most. Grandpa was used to say that his
father had instructed William Kent to design these
windows in such a way that he might the better
appreciate that particular corner of his grace's deer
park."

As she spoke, her mouth curved into a smile
that made Mrs. Windlesham reflect quite crossly
upon the turn of fate that had left Perdita, at six
and twenty, still a spinster and likely to remain so,
for all that she was as beautiful a young woman as
you might hope to find anywhere—if one could
indeed call it a turn of fate. Pure selfishness, more
like!

It did not behoove one to think ill of the dead, but as she had confided to Mr. Windlesham only that morning, what else was it but selfishness that had prompted Sir Edwin to keep Perdita tied to his side instead of making a push to see her happily settled? "And you need not tell me that the opportunity did not arise, for I myself twice offered to chaperon her for a London Season the year after Lucy's come-out!"

Her husband's mild recollection that it had been Perdita herself who had declined this generous offer had put Mrs. Windlesham out of all patience with him.

"And what does a young gel know of such matters, pray? With no woman to guide her except Almeria Midgely, who for all her excellent qualities is not in the least bit sophisticated. Small wonder that Perdita was so ready to accept that her world was bounded by the confines of Bath!"

But Sir Edwin knew different, she mused, and no one would ever convince her otherwise. And here was Perdita thinking that the sun shone out of him—it put one out of all patience! Her bright darting glance had not missed the traces of recent tears, though she would not dream of alluding to them.

"Speaking of the duke, my love," she said confidentially, "I fear that his leg has been troubling him a great deal. Dr. Bryant was obliged to call at Anderley Court twice on Tuesday, and was to go again on Wednesday after he had visited Clarissa."

Perdita was at once filled with guilt. "I knew he should not have gone to the funeral, but he and Grandpa had become such good friends of late. They were very much alike, you know, in that there was no holding either of them once they took a notion into their heads! I really must go to him. He will be thinking me shockingly ungrateful!"

"Nonsense, my dear child, I'm sure his grace will think nothing of the kind. In the circumstances he cannot have expected you to call." Mrs. Windlesham could see that Perdita was not convinced, and sought to divert her attention from morbid reflection. "I believe young Mr. Gilles attempted to visit yesterday afternoon, and was informed by Pendlebury that the duke was not well enough to receive callers." Her mouth quivered into a smile that was just faintly tinged with malice. "Poor man! I think he would have liked to protest that as a man of the cloth it was his duty to minister to the sick, but I fear that his grace's butler intimidates him almost as much as the duke himself!"

This drew a chuckle from Perdita. "I believe Pendlebury has been with the duke forever, so I suppose it is inevitable that some of his grace's high-nosed ways have rubbed off on him." She sobered. "But I am sorry that the duke is unwell."

By the time Mrs. Windlesham left, Perdita found that any lingering determination to write letters had left her. She went upstairs and changed her sober gown for the riding habit of dark gray cloth frogged in black velvet which had been her first priority when considering mourning dress. To be unable to ride for lack of a suitable garment would have cast her deeper into gloom than ever, and that, she persuaded herself, would not have pleased her grandfather. As for her hat—the high-crowned black shako which sat her fair hair so elegantly, its exceedingly dashing peak perched over her eyes, would doubtless be frowned on by some, not least because of a military-style tuft of feathers which had caused even Midge's eyes to open rather wider than usual. She pulled on her gloves of tan kid with a touch of defiance.

She came downstairs to find Fletcher already in

the hall. "It is too pleasant by far to remain indoors, and besides I feel very much in need of some fresh air," she told him as he went before her to open the side door leading to the stables. "If Miss Midgely should return before I do, tell her that I have ridden across to Anderley Court to inquire after his grace."

Chapter 3

*I*T MIGHT WELL HAVE astonished Mrs. Windle-sham to learn that Perdita, for all her apparent serenity, did occasionally look to the future with misgivings. During her grandfather's lifetime her fears had been minimal and easy to subdue, for they had enjoyed a tremendous regard for each other and pleasure in each other's company that had quite transcended the disparity in age. Time enough, she had thought then with the careless-ness of the young, in whom each moment is sa-vored of itself without heed for the morrow.

Now as she traversed her own orchards and rode down toward the unofficial path she had worn through the woodland that bounded the Duke of Anderley's parkland, the future suddenly looked depressingly flat. So many of the pastimes she had enjoyed in Sir Edwin's company—the weekend hunting parties in season, Newmarket for the races, and summer visits to Brighton—and even, since the peace in Europe, the occasional continental tour—most of these would be as good as barred to a single young woman, even to one chaperoned by someone as impeccably upright as Almeria Midgely. The best Perdita could hope for would be an invitation to some innocuous house party where she would be very much the lone spinster; anything of a more adventurous nature would surely be considered more than a trifle *fast*, and though this would not bother her, it would most certainly appall Midge.

For the first time she found herself wondering whether she might not have made rather better use of past opportunities. How lightly she had turned down Mrs. Windlesham's offer to sponsor her for a London Season all those years back, only because Grandpa had hated London, and she knew how much he would miss her if she went without him. There had, of course, been the assemblies in Bath which she had attended regularly with that same lady. She had not been without admirers there; indeed, Mrs. Windlesham vowed that she might have had her pick of any one of several young men much taken by her fair beauty and engaging openness of manner, but since no gentleman had ever come within Perdita's orbit who could make her pulses stir, let along leap with even a modicum of that romantical desire so frequently experienced by the heroines she had encountered between the pages of books, she had for the most part grown philosophical. Her only proposal had come from Bertram, and he had so obviously been motivated by the necessity to shore up his perilous financial state that she had been able to refuse him without a qualm.

The trees had by now given place to open parkland, and presently the house came into view, elegantly sprawling in the late-spring sunshine, which lent the honey-colored Bath stone an added warmth. It was not a large house by aristocratic standards, but then the estate itself was not sizable, being one of the Duke of Anderley's lesser properties. Until recent times it had been occupied by the duke's wife, now deceased.

Perdita had probably known the duchess as well as anyone hereabouts ever knew her, for as a child she had ventured many a time into the Anderley woods in pursuit of pleasures not to be found in the more formal gardens of her own home. And occasionally she had met the strange foreign lady wandering there with her pets. She was an odd reclusive woman who had loved animals better than people, and kept seven dogs, a parrot, and a pet monkey, the last being allowed to sit at table with her, striking terror into the servants by biting them with distressing frequency.

Mrs. Windlesham had often owned to a decided curiosity to learn how his grace had come to marry her in the first place, "for they are not in the least alike, my love," she had once confided to Perdita in hushed gossiping tones. "Of course, the most likely explanation is that she somehow entrapped him whilst he was still grieving over the loss of his first wife."

This had surprised Perdita. "I didn't know . . ."

"That she was not his first wife? Oh no, my dear. The first duchess was altogether different! Such a beautiful creature she was . . . and he, for all his rakish ways, head over ears in love with her! But they had not been married a twelvemonth when she, poor child—for she was not much more—died giving birth to their son. The duke was distraught, and for a while went quite wild, cut himself off from all his friends."

"Oh, the poor man!" Perdita exclaimed softly.

"Well, of course it was quite tragic, but when someone refuses to be helped . . ." Mrs. Windlesham shrugged. "It all seems a very long time ago, now."

"What happened to the child?" Perdita had wanted to know.

"He was given into the care of his grace's elder sister, who took him to the family's country seat in Warwickshire, and nothing more was heard of the duke for several years, not in fact until he returned from abroad with his new duchess on his arm. It very quickly became apparent that his second marriage was no love match, and any hopes that the little marquis might look forward to having a new mama were set at naught when, instead of taking his bride to Warwickshire, his grace brought her here. And here she remained, keeping very much to herself ... an odd woman, you must agree."

"I wonder why he *did* marry her."

"Oh, there were rumors enough at the time, some of them less than savory, I believe, but his grace seemed impervious to the tattle-mongering. He returned to London and resumed his old ways, embarking upon a succession of mistresses ... high-fliers that soon made his name a byword!"

At which point, Mrs. Windlesham had suddenly recollected that such frankness was not for the ears of an eighteen-year-old girl, and had attempted to change the subject. But there had been one thing more Perdita longed to know.

"And his son?"

"St. Ive? Oh, my dear, if all I hear is but half true, he is already well on the way to rivaling his father's reputation. So sad after all his aunt did for him!"

The story had intrigued Perdita. She tried often to conjure a picture of the duke, and had even resorted to quizzing her grandfather, who had revealed somewhat surprisingly that he had been at Oxford with his grace and had liked him rather well in those days, though he showed every sign even then of becoming a rakehell.

And then about a year ago they had met the duke at a weekend shooting party given by mutual friends and she saw at once that stories about him had not been exaggerated. He was, even in his sixtieth year, a devastatingly attractive man, the kind of man that women must always find irresistible, in spite of, or perhaps because of, his reputation.

Their paths had crossed several times thereafter, and he and Sir Edwin had resumed the friendship forged at Oxford—two men so different in some ways, so alike in others. And then, at a Boxing Day meet not twenty miles from Bath, the duke's horse had stumbled on the frost-hard ground and thrown his rider. Perdita had been just behind him when he fell. She had rendered him what assistance she could, and had stayed with him until the grooms arrived with a gate upon which they bore him away cursing, and clearly in great pain.

A grueling session with the local doctor, who had diagnosed a broken ankle, ended with the unfortunate man being ejected almost forcibly from his grace's presence, following upon his suggestion that the duke should be bled, after which he dispatched his man to arrange for Anderley Court to be opened up, the staff from his London residence installed, and his traveling coach sent to convey him there with all speed. And there he had been for the last four months, a prey to frustration, his ankle slow to recover from the mauling it had received initially.

Throughout that time, Perdita had been one of the few people whose company was unfailingly welcome. Pendlebury, his grace's butler, had been heard to say on more than one occasion that no matter how cross-grained the duke might be, Miss

Grant could be relied upon to tease him into a better humor.

She gave her mount into the charge of the boy who came running from the stableyard to meet her, and then walked across the wide lawns to where a series of terraced walks led up to a garden room which adjoined a suite of rooms made over to the duke's requirements so that he would have no stairs to negotiate. It was here that the duke was most often to be found on sunny days.

Perdita had formed the habit of entering informally at his express command, and now as always she was aware of the restfulness of the garden room with its greenery and a small fountain splashing water into the shallow pool where every now and then a red-gold shape stirred and there came the iridescent flash of a tall fin.

"Good afternoon, Perdita. So you have come at last," said the Duke of Anderley from the chaise longue where he was presently obliged to spend so much of his time. The heavily bandaged foot which held him captive did not, however, detract one iota from the grandeur of his appearance—his brocade dressing robe much embellished with black silk frogging, and his white hair pomaded and tied back in a queue, looking very much as it must have done when, as a young man, he had worn it *en poudre*.

Perdita's eyes were twinkling as she hurried forward, but her smile faded into concern as she stretched out her hands to him.

"My dear sir! Mrs. Windlesham informs me that you have been laid low. I feared that the funeral might have proved too much for you. Does your leg pain you very much?"

"Damnably." Deep-set blue eyes under heavy lids gleamed balefully in a face hewn into strong classical lines and dominated by an awesome nose.

"But if you mean to heed the fictions of that gabble-grinding woman, and have come to address me as though I were at my last prayers, you may return home now on the instant, and leave me to my own devices."

He spoke in the clipped tones of someone who is driven as much by frustration as pain, and since he showed no inclination to release his grip on her hands, she made herself comfortable on the stool beside him.

"Is that why you turned poor Mr. Gilles from your door?" she asked lightly.

"Sanctimonious prig! My reprehensible past sticks in his teeth, but he knows full well that any hope of advancement would fly out the window if he lost my patronage, so he takes refuge in unctuous rhetoric!"

"Well, you cannot blame him for that. A curate's stipend is little more than adequate, after all, and if he has any ambition at all, you can hardly expect him to throw his chances away over what he must recognize as a lost cause!"

The duke uttered a derisive grunt. "You're mighty quick to his defense, madam. You don't favor that block of clerical rectitude, I hope?"

Perdita's laughter spilled out. "No, but I suspect he wishes I might!"

"Well, I give you fair warning—you'll forfeit my friendship an' you do." But there was a gleam in his eye that took the sting from the threat.

"I can see that it's high time I came back to humanize you," said Perdita. "You have grown monstrously uncivil in my absence." She sighed and dropped her teasing. "Indeed, I am sorry to have neglected you so badly in these last few days, but in truth there has been so much to do."

"Been bad, has it?" She shrugged expressively, and he squeezed her hands and gave them back to her, his drawl more than usually pronounced as he said, "Your grandfather was quite a man. You're bound to miss him. At all events, that cousin of yours is gone back to London, so I hear. Best place for him."

Perdita told him about Bertram's letter.

The duke grunted. "Running true to type. I know Edwin thought him a loose fish. Told me once that Tillot's father was a ne'er-do-well. Let me know if the fellow makes a nuisance of himself."

She smiled at him. "Thank you, my dear friend, but I took Cousin Bertram's measure a long time ago. He was a bad loser, even as a child, so I am fairly adept at handling his quirks by now."

For a moment Perdita feared that she had said the wrong thing. The duke pokered up, his profile stiff with pride. Might he perhaps have taken her reply to imply that she thought him now incapable of helping her? She leaned forward and rushed again into speech.

"I'm sorry, that sounded ungrateful, and indeed I did not mean it to be. You may be sure that at the least hint of trouble, I shall not hesitate to call upon you!"

For a moment his expression did not alter appreciably. Then he turned to look at her. "You're a good girl." He tapped her cheek lightly. "I have missed you."

From behind her, a strange voice drawled, "An affecting little scene. Do I intrude?"

Perdita swung around to see a tall young man with an air of swashbuckling arrogance that she found vaguely familiar lounging against the door leading to the drawing room and surveying them with eyeglass raised. His buckskins fitted like a second skin, his riding coat had been cut by a master, and his neckcloth was arranged with a flourish, all of which added up to that indefinable quality Mrs. Windlesham would term "London polish." How long he had been there, she knew not, so silently had he come. Bereft of speech, she turned to the duke and found him coldly formal.

"Miss Grant, allow me to make my son, St. Ive, known to you."

The marquis bowed with exquisite formality. She was prevented from rising to make her curtsy by the duke's hand, which had once more imprisoned one of hers with a possessiveness amounting almost to truculence which at any other time she might have found amusing. As it was, she was obliged to return the marquis's greeting with a polite inclination of the head.

"My son has, it seems, been so filled with concern about my continuing indisposition that he has finally made some time in his busy life to come and see for himself how I am progressing. I must be grateful, I suppose, that it has taken him but four months to do so!"

The sarcasm found its mark. The marquis flushed, and just for a moment the two men were so alike that Perdita was astonished that she had not immediately perceived it—the same indolent grace and strongly classical features, the same raking intimacy in the hard brilliance of the blue, deep-set eyes which in the father she was able to meet with tolerable composure, even a certain amusement, but which in the son brought an embarrassed warmth to her cheeks.

That their temperaments were also similar became obvious as the marquis recovered himself to say with studied ambiguity, "On the contrary, sir, you might be surprised to learn how much I have your interests at heart!" His glance rested momentarily on his father before moving on to his companion.

"Indeed?" the duke returned coldly, his hand

tightening on Perdita's. "Such filial concern must surely rejoice any father's heart. Wouldn't you agree, my dear?"

But Perdita was fast reaching exasperation point; aware that whatever her reply, it must sound either censorious or evasive, she had no desire to figure as a kind of verbal shuttlecock to be tossed back and forth between father and son. She gave a determined little tug to release her hands and stood up, eyeing the duke reproachfully.

"I am really not qualified to give an opinion, your grace," she said crisply. "And in any case, I must go." She could not forbear to add waspishly, "You will be wishing to have your son to yourself, I daresay, since you see him so seldom."

The duke's dry chuckle betrayed his appreciation of this thrust. "You'll come again soon?"

"Yes, of course, dear sir. And pray don't tire yourself with too much talking." She dropped a light kiss on his forehead, and there was just the suspicion of a challenge in her eyes as she bade the marquis a formal goodbye. "I will leave the way I came."

THERE WAS SILENCE as the door closed behind her.

"So that is Miss Grant," St. Ive said softly. "She seems deucedly at home here."

"As she has every right to be. I owe Perdita a great deal—more than I can easily repay."

"I see," murmured his son.

"Do you, Piers?" the duke said coolly. "I doubt it. You will not have met anyone quite like her among your friends, I think. Not," he added, "that I have the least obligation to explain Perdita to you, but I'll tell you this much—she is worth ten of any woman I've ever met, bar one. She was at my side within moments of my taking that damnable toss and behaved with a coolness and presence of mind that impressed me considerably. And that wasn't the end of it, either. She insisted upon bearing me company on the journey home in the hope of easing my discomfort, though I can hardly have been the easiest of traveling companions! And she has visited me with unfailing cheerfulness ever since, as did her grandfather until his recent death."

"A veritable paragon," observed St. Ive.

"It may please you to sneer, my boy, but the Grants and one or two others have been a Godsend to me! I only hope you may never find yourself laid up for so long. Life becomes insupportably tedious, I can tell you. You would be surprised how many so-called friends melt away when one is out of circulation for any length of time."

"Perhaps you don't precisely encourage them to visit," St. Ive mused, half to himself. And then, looking up to meet his father's eyes, "Forgive me if I am frank, sir, but you are not always the most approachable of men."

"Don't be mealy-mouthed, Piers. I have no illusions as to your opinion of me. We never have dealt together, and there's an end of it."

The duke's voice was brusque, and St. Ive saw that his father had grown rather white about the mouth.

"You are in pain," he said abruptly. "I'm sorry—I shouldn't have let you go on talking for so long."

"Don't fuss, for the love of God!" snapped the duke. "That's another excellent quality Perdita has. She never fusses! You could do worse than emulate her!"

"Thank you. I'll try to remember," returned his son, equally tight-lipped as he strode to the door.

PERDITA WAS ALMOST HALFWAY down the drive when she realized she was being followed. Her first instinct urged her to break into a gallop; only a

strong conviction that the marquis would successfully pursue her induced wiser councils to prevail.
"Easy, Satan," she murmured, running a soothing
hand down her horse's sleek neck as she slowed
him to a walk to allow his lordship to catch up.

"Miss Grant. A moment, if you please."

The peremptory voice was not encouraging, but
she waited civilly enough for St. Ive to draw level.
His big rangy gelding unsettled Satan, but after
allowing him to caracol playfully for a moment she
very quickly brought him under control, so that he
stood just flicking a watchful eye at the other
horse.

"Very impressive," St. Ive said grudgingly, ob-
serving the ease with which she sat the powerful
black hunter. "But he is hardly a lady's mount,
surely?"

"It depends on the lady," she replied equably.

"But of course." One eyebrow lifted sardonically.
"I had forgot. The intrepid Miss Grant is a bruising
rider to hounds."

Perdita felt exasperation rising and strove to quell
it. "I can't imagine where you came by that notion,
my lord!"

"Simple deduction, Miss Grant. My father told
me that you were at his side almost as soon as he
fell, and he always prides himself on being well up
with the field—ergo, you must also have been well
to the fore."

She acknowledged the quickness of his reasoning with a reluctant smile. It brought no answer
beyond a kind of inscrutable stare. She sat a little
straighter and stared back.

"Well, sir?" she said at last when he made no
attempt to break the silence. "I presume you came
after me for a purpose?"

If she hoped to disconcert him, there was no

evidence that she had succeeded. Nor did he make any direct attempt to answer her question.

"My father owes you quite a debt, it would appear," he said in that deceptively lazy voice.

"I do hope not!" she exclaimed. "I can think of nothing more tiresome than to be regarded as an object of gratitude. I did only what anyone would have done in my place."

"Oh, surely not, ma'am—you are too modest by far. Not everyone would have carried her ministrations to such ends! Supervising everything, including his journey here, paying him frequent visits . . ." He paused significantly. "You do visit him often, do you not?"

"Most days." Perdita met his glance squarely, though she could not for the life of her see why she should feel obliged to explain her behavior. "The duke feels his inactivity very keenly. I don't know if he has told you, but his ankle has not healed as it should . . . the doctor who treated him originally was appallingly cow-handed! I sometimes suspect that his grace shares my own fear that it will never again bear his weight." Compassion was very evident in her voice as she concluded, "But I have not broached the possibility, and I beg that you will not do so either! So long as it remains unsaid, there is still room for pride—and hope. As to my visits—they seem to please him; he is very much alone, you know, except for the servants and a very few neighboring friends."

The marquis had been watching her face, which had become more than a little animated. "And is that how you like to see yourself—as my father's friend?"

There was an inflection in the words that jarred on her—a deep underlying irony that carried a hint of menace. Or was she being overfanciful? Whatever the explanation, she was by now in no mood to be intimidated.

"I should be honored to think he regarded me as a friend," she said with an angry flippancy that Miss Midgely would have deplored, "and I'm sorry if the thought displeases you. To be honest, I cannot see why it should matter to you one way or the other, since you obviously care so little for his grace that you have not come near him until now!"

It had been her avowed intention to embarrass him, and a twitching muscle close to his mouth seemed to suggest that she had succeeded. When she looked into his eyes she was sure of it.

"My feelings toward my father are none of your business, madam." His voice was silky-soft. "Had I known what was going on, however, I might well have come sooner."

Perdita's hands tightened on the reins, causing Satan to back nervously. Her voice as she gentled him totally belied the challenge in her eyes.

"My lord, I have a great dislike of ambiguity, so we will have plain speaking, if you please. You are clearly laboring under some misapprehension with regard to my visits to his grace, though for the life of me I cannot fathom it."

St. Ive marveled that anyone so fair and pleasing to the eye could be so . . . devious! "Plain speaking, you say. But what of your sensibilities, Miss Grant?"

"I have none, sir."

In a tree above their heads a pigeon was cooing—a repetitive mocking sound that seemed to echo the underlying tensions, which also communicated themselves to the marquis's horse, so that it in turn grew restive. St. Ive brought its head around with ruthless authority, his voice grating suddenly.

"Very well, ma'am. But tell me first of all—how do you see my father?"

"Oh really! I cannot possibly . . ."

"Come now," he pressed her. "Is he not a romantic figure? A peer of the highest degree—a man whose past is strewn with women of all ages and all shades of respectability. Such a reputation must even now lend him an aura of . . . tantalizing allure? And you have him here, captive—yours the hand that smooths his brow, yours the smile to charm him back into humor when he is fractious! What an opportunity, Miss Grant, for a young and unattached woman of sense, if not sensibility, to turn the situation to her advantage!"

Perdita could not believe what she was hearing. His cutting condemnation within so short a time of meeting her seemed so unjust that she was unsure if she could trust herself to speak. Her fingers, curling convulsively round her riding crop, were itching to strike at his handsome arrogant face. Instead, she schooled her voice to equal his coldness.

"I fear you must make your argument still plainer, my lord. Of what exactly do I stand accused—infatuation or opportunism?"

Not simply devious, he thought. Miss Perdita Grant was, unequivocally, brass-faced! "I would not presume to hazard the degree of your attachment, ma'am, but it is quite obvious to me that you have been at considerable pains to make yourself indispensable to my father."

The sheer idiocy of his accusation momentarily overcame her anger, and she laughed in his face. "And it is equally clear to me, my lord, that you have windmills in your head. I have nothing further to say to you except to bid you good day."

She gathered up the reins and turned to move off, but he was after her in a flash, his hand shooting out to seize her bridle. "Not so fast, Miss Grant. I haven't anywhere near finished with you yet."

Perdita was horrified to find that she was shaking; the strain of the past few weeks, the worry and the grief that she had so successfully contained, came boiling to the surface in a kind of incoherent rage. For once she was without defenses, not caring if she seemed foolish or unreasonable, or even hysterical, not caring that her voice was shrill and trembled pathetically, just as long as she could free herself from this insufferable man.

"But I have finished with you, my lord! I have tried to be patient with you for your father's sake, but in the light of your hostility I c-cannot believe he would wish me to suffer your ill manners one m-moment more!" She began to tug at the rein. "Now, *let me go!*"

"I will do so when I have your assurance that any designs you may have upon my father will cease forthwith."

Designs! Dear God! She said through her teeth, "And if I do not care to do so?"

He seemed to be weighing his words. "Then I must take whatever measures seem appropriate to protect my father."

Perdita looked into his ice-cold blue eyes and saw that he meant it. Inexplicably, the knowledge of it had a calming effect upon her—as though the lines had been drawn and battle declared.

"Then perhaps you will also explain to his grace why, after exhibiting such a complete disregard for his welfare, you are suddenly so worried that he might be contemplating a *mésalliance*," she said without taking her eyes from his. "He might be inclined to wonder as I do whether it is his happiness that concerns you, or a desire to protect your inheritance!"

"Oh, you cunning jade!" he exclaimed with soft vehemence.

At last she had pierced his armor. She felt a sense of elation beyond all reason. And though he recovered his composure at once, she knew that for now at least she had won. Without a word she allowed her glance to move pointedly from his eyes to the hand grasping her bridle, and then back again. For a moment it seemed that he would attempt to stare her out of countenance. Then he shrugged, removed his hand, and said almost pleasantly, "Very well, Miss Grant, you may go. But don't be tempted to rejoice. This is by no means the end of it!"

Chapter 4

BY THE TIME Perdita arrived home she was once more in full command of her emotions, but her calmness was a fragile thing, not yet to be trusted, so she resolutely drove from her mind any temptation to dwell upon recent events. As she came through into the hall, she was met by Fletcher with the news that Mr. Gilles was in the drawing room.

"He arrived about ten minutes since, Miss Perdita," the butler went on in his most noncommittal manner, "and was seemingly quite cast down to find that you were from home. Miss Midgely, having but a short time before returned from Bath, suggested that he might care to take a little refreshment in the expectation that you must soon be home."

Drat Midge, she thought, knowing there would be no escape. "Thank you, Fletcher," she said, matching him for equivocality. "How very kind of Miss Midgely."

"Quite so, ma'am." They exchanged a glance of complete understanding.

It wasn't precisely that Midge saw Mr. Gilles as a desirable suitor, she reflected with a brief flash of humor as she made her way unhurriedly to the drawing room. But it did vex her ex-governess that Perdita had squandered the many respectable opportunities afforded her over recent years with what she was wont to term a willful disregard for the future. "The day will come," she never tired of warning Perdita, "when you could find yourself obliged to cut your coat according to the available cloth if you are not to languish forever in spinsterhood." And though she still dreamed of a fine match, Perdita suspected that when Mr. Gilles had arrived just over a year ago to take up the living at Anderley church, Midge had put a mental tag on him—*clerical gentleman of good character and unexceptional looks, not much above thirty, unencumbered and ambitious for advancement. Under consideration.* To which Perdita was inclined to add her own appendage—*but only if desperate.*

The smile was still lingering in her eyes when she entered the drawing room and advanced to greet the said neatly dressed clerical gentleman, who stood up hurriedly, setting down his cup with a clatter on the small table beside him, and in his eagerness slopping tea into the saucer.

"Miss Grant—oh, this is splendid! I had begun to fear that I should not have the pleasure of seeing you!" He indicated his own chair. "Do, pray, come and sit down near the fire. I am sure you must be tired and chilled from your ride, for all that the fresh air has brought some color back to your cheeks."

"No, truly, I shall do very well over here," she protested in amusement. "I am not in the least tired. In fact, I hadn't realized how much I was in need of the exercise!"

Perdita stripped off her gloves and removed the jaunty black riding hat and tossed them carelessly onto a chair while Mr. Gilles stifled unworthy thoughts concerning the hat's unsuitability as mourning apparel and struggled to equate his image of a grieving Miss Grant with this smiling creature glowing with health.

He continued to hover, the epitome of solid worth allied to impeccable manners, until Perdita had accepted a teacup from Miss Midgely and had made herself comfortable on a nearby sofa. She noted inconsequentially as he sat down again that he had the beginnings of a double chin.

"How kind of you to spare time from your busy round to come and visit us," she said at last, "when you must have many more urgent duties to fulfill."

"Nothing of the sort, dear ma'am," he was quick to reassure her. "Oh, I am always busy, of course—my little flock to tend, poor creatures—some of them, I fear, not fully resigned to the will of God—"

He sighed heavily, and Perdita restrained with considerable effort the temptation to tell him that he might find it equally difficult to resign himself to the acute poverty that was the lot of so many of his flock. A warning cough from Miss Midgely finally decided her. She shrugged and sat back.

"But never, I hope," continued Mr. Gilles, sublimely unaware of any hint of discord in the air, "so busy that I would neglect to satisfy myself of your well-being, especially following so soon upon your tragic loss. You may be sure that I account such a visitation as much more than mere duty!"

The warm look that accompanied this assurance was so marked that there could be no mistaking its meaning. She became very busy stirring her tea as the older woman deftly changed the subject.

"Mr. Gilles is the bearer of the most diverting item of news, my dear. How fortunate that you will be able to give us confirmation of it. He tells me that the duke's son is come to Anderley Court?"

"It's true," Perdita said shortly, not wishing to be reminded of the marquis.

"There now!" exclaimed Mr. Gilles. "So Mrs. Windlesham was not mistaken! I met her as she was returning to Bath after visiting you, dear Miss Grant. Quite shaken she was, poor lady, full of having had her barouche-landau almost forced off the road by his lordship's curricle as it swept past her and turned in at the gates of Anderley Court!"

How like St. Ive! Perdita mused wrathfully. No consideration whatever for other road-users! So absorbed was she in this silent vilification that she was not aware of the curious glance directed at her by Miss Midgely.

"Did you meet the marquis, Perdita?"

"I did," she said, the light of battle still in her eyes. "But if you do not wish me to be unchristian, pray don't ask me for my opinion of him."

"Dear me, how fierce you sound, Miss Grant! One has heard rumors, of course, and I am sure it is not to be wondered at if his lordship is a trifle wild, with the example of his father's conduct ever before him."

But this was going too far for Perdita. "My quarrel is with St. Ive's manners, not his morals," she said with a frankness and asperity that took him back a little and made him wonder whether he was perhaps being unwise in allowing his heart to rule his head. His uneasiness grew as she continued, "And I fail to see how his grace can be held responsible for those, or rather the lack of them, when he had little or nothing to do with his upbringing! The duke may have been a regular rakehell in his day, but I have always found *his* manners to be impeccable!"

Mr. Gilles felt he had outstayed his welcome. He stood up, his face a trifle flushed. "Where you are concerned, I am sure they always are, ma'am, but it is not always the case, I promise you!"

What he had intended as a mild reproof succeeded only in sounding pettish, and Perdita, remembering that only a day or so before he had himself received short shrift at Anderley Court, was immediately racked with guilt. It brought her impulsively to her feet.

"I'm sure you are right, sir, and I should not have taken my irritation out on you. Forgive me. My tongue does occasionally run away with me."

He was immediately mollified. "Pray think nothing of it, my dear Miss Grant. I entirely understand that you are not feeling quite yourself at present. You put on such a brave face that one is inclined to forget!"

"Oh lordy, Midge," she groaned when he had gone. "I do hope he won't construe my apology as an invitation to pursue his expectations!"

"If he does, you will be well served," said Almeria Midgely in her most forthright tones. "Whatever was all that nonsense about Lord St. Ive?"

Perdita shrugged. "Oh, that—it was nothing. I just didn't take to his lordship, that's all."

Perdita knew she was being evasive, but at that moment she felt quite unequal to the task of trying to explain St. Ive's addle-headed notions, with all the attendant probing from Midge that would ensue. She could only hope that his lordship would soon tire of country life and return to the dizzy pleasures of London. Meanwhile, she must nerve herself to call again at Anderley Court, if only to prove to him that she would not be intimidated. But in the event, her brave posturing was all for nothing.

"Driven into Bath, my dear," said the duke. "To renew an old acquaintance, if you please. I'd have thought any friend of Piers's would find Bath much too slow, but there . . ."

*   *   *

THE MARQUIS WAS at that moment being admitted to a house in Great Pulteney Street, where, after a small delay, he was ushered up to the drawing room. A young woman whose dark lustrous curls encompassed a face of delicate beauty rose from a sofa near the window, her voice betraying a thread of tremulous uncertainty.

"Lord St. Ive! I had not expected . . . that is to say, what a delightful surprise!"

"Amaryllis." He captured the hand half extended toward him and planted an unhurried kiss in its palm. "Can it be possible? You are even more lovely than I remember!"

Her breath caught adorably as she pulled her hand away. "No . . . really, you must not say such things to me now that I am a married lady!"

"Must I not?" His eyes darkened momentarily. Then a wry smile touched his mouth. "So be it, *Lady Munro!*" He made her a bow. "But you can't stop me thinking as I please!" He watched with interest the color run up under her skin. "How is Harry?"

"*Very* well," she exclaimed with enthusiasm. "Oh, please . . . will you not sit down? I am not quite used yet to entertaining. Mama was always used to take care of such things so splendidly! But Harry says I shall soon learn the way of it! If only we had known you were in Bath . . . you have come to see your father, I suppose. Harry has only gone to Twerton to visit his grandmother. He will be so sorry to have missed you, but perhaps if you mean to stay a few days, there will be an opportunity to meet later. He would so enjoy hearing all the *on-dits*."

St. Ive, sitting facing her with every appearance of ease, was somewhat disconcerted to discover that marriage had already invested her with an extra bloom; he would have been better pleased to find her pale, and pining just a little for all that she had thrown over for love.

"Are you happy?" he asked abruptly.

"Oh, indeed, yes!" she declared.

"And you don't miss London?" He would have liked to add *and me*, but in the face of such shining happiness, he felt that the question must lack relevance.

She shook her head, and the dark curls danced. "Hardly at all. There are so many agreeable things to do here! I have made any number of new friends—"

"And have already quite forgotten your old ones?" he finished for her with sudden questioning intentness.

"No! That is . . ." Amaryllis was thrown into fresh confusion by his manner—the way he had of looking at one as though no one else existed for him, so that one was scared and excited all at the same time. But she had chosen Harry, she reminded herself with a kind of despairing panic— she *loved* Harry, dear Harry who was kind and thoughtful and worshiped her, and with whom she felt safe. So how could it be that there was a tiny part of her that still melted at the sight, the mere closeness, of St. Ive? Oh, if only Harry were here now . . . if only she had not been so unwise as to receive Lord St. Ive alone! Panic threatened anew, and as the little clock on the mantelshelf struck she sprang to her feet.

"Oh goodness, how silly of me! With your coming I had quite forgot . . . I promised to visit Mrs. Windlesham, in Sydney Place. She must be wondering where I am!"

His lazy eyes held the hint of a smile as he too rose and stood looking down at her. How transparent she was—how easy it would be to woo her away from her husband should he so wish it.

"I'll take you," he said softly, and as her eyes widened, "To Mrs. Windlesham's," he added with blandness. "It's years since we last met."

"You know Mrs. Windlesham?" Amaryllis asked faintly.

"We are—distantly acquainted," he murmured.

A number of people were gathered in the Windlesham drawing room when the new arrivals were admitted. A faint ripple of interest ran around the room as Mrs. Windlesham bustled forward to greet them.

"Lady Munro, what a very pleasant surprise! So you did not go to Twerton with Sir Henry after all?"

Amaryllis scarcely knew where to look, but anywhere would suffice, so long as it was not at her companion, whose amusement she could sense.

"N-no, I had the headache," she stammered, coloring. "You do not mind my bringing Lord St. Ive, dear ma'am? He arrived quite unexpectedly, and when I told him that it had been my intention to visit you, he expressed a wish to renew his acquaintance with you."

"Mind? My dear child, I couldn't be more pleased!" Mrs. Windlesham exclaimed. "You are very welcome, my lord. Do pray come and let me make you known to Lady Brinkley and her daughter, Maria. Lady Brinkley, here is Lord St. Ive, who is come to Bath, I have no doubt, to visit his poor father. Am I not right, my lord?"

He inclined his head and admitted that it was indeed concern for his parent that had prompted his present appearance in Bath. Such very proper filial sentiments clearly found favor among Mrs. Windlesham's guests. General Gorey was heard to comment to Miss Prothero that he was much heartened by this evidence of regard in the younger generation, and Mrs. Windlesham's generous bosom swelled with pride as she savored the accolade of St. Ive's presence. Nothing, she was sure, could be more guaranteed to please than his coat of dove-gray superfine, fashioned by a master, the pale pantaloons and gleaming Hessians; nothing more handsome than his lordship's willingness to mingle, and with no more condescension than might be considered proper in the circumstances, some of which might well be due to his rather hawklike profile.

It was as well, perhaps, that Mrs. Windlesham could not read his lordship's mind, for he was at that precise moment wondering what had possessed him to land himself in such tedious company, and coming to the rueful conclusion that he was well served for seeking to exploit his influence over Amaryllis.

"And how do you find the duke's health, my lord?" came the thin voice of Lady Brinkley.

"Less robust than I had hoped for, ma'am," he replied. "I suspect his ankle gives him a great deal of pain."

"A bad business," muttered the general.

Miss Prothero's reedy voice rose clearly above the murmurs of agreement. "He is fortunate, however, is he not, in that he has Miss Grant to tend him and help him while away his tedium? I have heard it said that even when Sir Edwin was on his deathbed, she found time to visit his grace!"

In the ensuing silence St. Ive fixed her with one of his most unfathomable stares. And it was into that silence that Amaryllis ventured impulsively to say, "Well, I think it was quite splendid of her! B-but it does not surprise me, for although we have not been very long acquainted, I already know Miss Grant to be just the kind of person on whom her friends may always depend, in the certain knowledge that she will be there when she is most needed! Wouldn't you say so, ma'am?"

Mrs. Windlesham threw her a look of deep gratitude. "Indeed I would, dear Lady Munro! I have known Perdita Grant for more than twenty years, and a more generous-natured girl I have yet to meet." She glared at Miss Prothero. "Anyone who says different will have me to answer to!"

Euphemia Prothero was a thin woman, as sharp of tongue as she was sharp-witted. Thus, she knew better than most how and when to employ her skills to best effect, and she sensed at once that now was not the place. But the seed had been sown, and his lordship's reaction had been curious, to say the least. Given time, Perdita Grant would pay for all the slights she and Sir Edwin had cast in her way.

As the conversation resumed, St. Ive leaned forward to quiz Amaryllis upon her brave defense of Miss Grant.

"I meant every word! If you did but know her, you would understand!"

"We—have met." One eyebrow quirked. "Somehow I don't see the two of you together."

Amaryllis grew a little pink, but held her ground. "Well, I'll own we are not quite of an age . . . and she is much cleverer than I, but she has shown me so much true kindness since I came to live in Bath! There are some things, you know, that even the best of husbands cannot be expected to know, and with Mama so far away . . ." At this point she became aware of several interested glances cast their way, and her explanation trailed away into incoherence, as fresh color flooded her face.

WHEN, TWO DAYS LATER, Perdita finally nerved herself to drive into Bath, she found St. Ive's name already on everyone's lips; further, to her dismay, she learned that it was being coupled with that of Lady Munro.

Perdita had known Harry Munro for many years, much of his childhood having been spent at Twerton with his maternal grandmother, Lady Frome, a formidable dowager whose brusque manners concealed a very genuine affection for the boy. She it was who had presented him with the house in Great Pulteney Street upon the occasion of his marriage, with the sole purpose, some said, of keeping Harry near her.

When Harry brought his bride to Bath after their honeymoon, Perdita was one of their first visitors. She had thought Amaryllis quite the loveliest creature she had ever seen, and quickly discovered her nature to be every bit as flawless as her looks. There was a gentle uncloying sweetness about her, an unstudied grace of movement, and just a hint of shyness in her manner that endeared her to all who met her. Harry quite clearly adored her, and she had eyes for no one but him. So how on earth, Perdita wondered, had she become involved with St. Ive?

The puzzle was partly explained by Mrs. Windlesham, whose barouche-landau drew up beside Perdita as she and Miss Midgely were about to enter Godwin's Circulating Library. The discovery of the pallid Clarissa shrinking into the corner, swamped by the flowing beneficence of her parent, occasioned much kind inquiry, after which Miss Midgely made her way into the library while Perdita remained to quiz Mrs. Windlesham.

"My dear, you may depend upon it, it was that silly Prothero woman and her careless tongue!" Mrs. Windlesham lowered her voice so that her daughter's ears migt not be assailed by disclosures of a somewhat delicate nature. "I'll not deny that I did think it a trifle singular when Lady Munro arrived at the first of my little afternoon receptions since Clarissa's illness on St. Ive's arm, when I was quite certain she had expressed to me her intention of going to Twerton with Sir Henry . . . although I know of course how much in awe of Lady Frome she is—"

"So Amaryllis actually came to your house *with* the marquis?"

"On his arm!" reiterated Mrs. Windlesham. "And one saw at once that they were not strangers to one another! I promise you, if it had been anyone but dear Lady Munro, my conclusions would have been much as anyone else's in the circumstances. But, sweet creature that she is, I am convinced that it was all perfectly innocent, and if he had been a complete nobody and something less than handsome, and if Euphemia Prothero had not sought to make much of little, the whole affair would have passed off as a five-minute wonder!"

At this point a diversion was caused by Miss Midgely's returning, triumphantly clasping her long-awaited copy of *Guy Mannering*, which encouraged Mrs. Windlesham to digress. She eyed the book with some disfavor, wrinkling her nose rather as though it were giving off an unpleasant odor.

"Mr. Windlesham vouches for its being very good," she said, "but I confess I am not in the least bookish and am more than willing to take his word on it. Naturally I have no objection to Clarissa's governess reading something of an improving nature aloud occasionally, though one could wish that she did not possess a voice more suited to declaiming dirges which frequently sends me to sleep! Still, that is neither here nor there, is it?"

Perdita, resigned to the fact that she would get nothing more that was at all to the point from her friend, absently murmured agreement, her mind already firmly fixed upon unraveling the next thread of the puzzle.

"We are on our way to the Pump Room, Perdita. I have determined to try if a short course of the waters will put a little color back in my poor Clarissa's cheeks. Dr. Bryant is not convinced that it will answer, being of the opinion that time and fresh air will take care of all, but I cannot stand to see her looking so pasty, and must at least make a push to do something!"

Perdita smiled sympathetically at Clarissa, in whom embarrassment at having attention thus focused upon her had given her pale face all the color it might wish for.

"Do you and Miss Midgely mean to come there also? I should be only too pleased to take you up."

It had been Perdita's intention so to do, but more important issues had now taken precedence. She turned to her companion. "Midge, do you go along with Mrs. Windlesham and Clarissa, and I will come to you presently." She resolutely resisted the look of reproach, saying beseechingly, "There is something very important that I must do!"

"But, my dear, you cannot mean to walk!" Mrs. Windlesham expostulated. "Only tell me where you wish to go and Jenkins shall convey you when he has put us down."

But Perdita only laughed and insisted that she was sorely in need of the exercise, which was why she had sent Silas with the carriage to await them in the Pump Room yard. She set off briskly in the direction of Great Pulteney Street, feeling the barbs of disapproval and ungratified curiosity boring into her back as she did so. As she came within sight of Harry Munro's house, she observed a familiar figure ahead of her on the opposite pavement. There was something almost furtive in the woman's indecisive hovering.

Unnoticed, Perdita crossed the road. "Miss Prothero—how extraordinary to meet you here! You are quite out of your way, surely?"

Miss Prothero started violently, but recovered almost at once. "Gracious! Miss Grant! One had not expected . . . that is to say, one might assume very much the same of you, surely?"

"Might one? I suppose so. But then I regularly come this way to visit friends."

"Even so," gushed the other, her darting eyes betraying veiled malevolence, "one can only marvel at your resilience in choosing to venture among us so soon, following upon your recent bereavement. I am sure that in your place I would have been prostrate for weeks!"

"Oh, Grandpa knocked that kind of missishness out of me at an early age," Perdita said lightly. "He had little time for what he called 'the pretentious claptrap of mourning,' and held strongly to the opinion that we could best demonstrate a true regard for our loved ones who have died by our care of the living." She looked squarely at Miss Prothero. "And I do think he was so right, don't you?"

"Sir Edwin was ever full of outlandish notions," snapped Miss Prothero, uncertainty about where the conversation might be leading making her quite forgetful of the ingratiating sentiments she had so recently committed to paper.

"Take my friends now—Sir Henry and Lady Munro—you will know them, of course. Poor Lady Munro has been the victim of some particularly cattish gossip, so I am come to give her what support I can. People can be very unkind." Perdita evinced an air of mild surprise. "Only fancy now—by happy coincidence, they live just across the road there, almost exactly opposite where we are standing now!"

Two spots of guilty color stood out in Miss

Prothero's cheeks as she ducked her head, drew her shawl closer about her bony shoulders, and murmured something about paying a chance visit to friends herself, and what a small world it was.

"Yes, isn't it?" Perdita agreed pleasantly. "You mustn't let me keep you here talking then. I do hope you will find your friends at home. It would be so tiresome for you, were you obliged to keep coming back on the off chance of catching them!" She nodded. "Good day, Miss Prothero."

Chapter 5

"OH, MY DEAR FRIEND, you can have no idea how pleased I am to see you!" Amaryllis exclaimed, and though her eyes lit up momentarily, Perdita was not slow to observe the slight catch in the soft husky voice, the dejected droop of the shoulders. She gave no sign, however, of having noticed anything amiss as they clasped hands.

"That is a new dress," she said approvingly, standing away a little. "And vastly becoming it is, too. I'll wager Harry had a hand in the choosing of it!" There was a fleeting look of misery in the younger woman's eyes at the mention of her husband, but Perdita continued with determined cheerfulness, "I wish I could wear sprigged muslin, but alas, I put such frivolities behind me several years ago." She grimaced. "Still, no matter. They would be of little use to me at present, after all!"

"Oh, how thoughtless I am!" Amaryllis's soft violet eyes were warm with compassion. "And how selfish to be permitting you to talk of trifles when you must be preoccupied with your grief!"

Perdita allowed herself to be fussed over and led to a sofa, but her manner remained determinedly cheerful. "If you must know, I am in flight from gloomy reflections. I was intending to visit the Pump Room, but the prospect of all those soulful looks and sympathetic utterances was suddenly more than I could face with equanimity! So I came to see my dear friends instead." Casually she added, "Where is Harry?"

At once Amaryllis sprang up and took a few agitated steps before standing very still, hands stiffly clasped before her, with her back to Perdita.

"He ... is in his room," she said in a stifled voice. "M-matters of business, he says ... but when he is not there, or out, he treats me politely ... like a stranger!" She spun around suddenly, her eyes swimming in tears. "Perdita, I have been so m-miserable!"

"My dear!" Perdita went immediately to put an arm around her, and in so doing, released the floodgates of despair. "Come now, this will not do!" she protested. "I suppose it is all the fault of that wretched man St. Ive! And the ubiquitous Miss Prothero! I found her hovering outside just now."

Amaryllis stopped in midsob to blink at her in surprise. "Then you know St. Ive ... and have doubtless heard what happened! Perdita, what am I to do?"

"I have heard nothing to merit so much misery! Oh, really, what an addle-brained creature Harry is, to be sure! What a piece of work to make over something and nothing!"

"No, no!" cried Amaryllis, springing to the defense of her beloved. "Indeed it is not that simple." She pulled herself together, wiped her eyes, and took a deep breath. "You see, when I met Harry, I was on the point of becoming betrothed to Lord St. Ive."

"Good gracious!"

"It was a match very much favored by Mama ... and I'll not deny that I was flattered by his attentions." The faint blush of guilt in her cheeks astonished Perdita. "Well, if you know him as I gather you must, you will surely be aware of his power to attract." She took Perdita's strangled utterance for assent and continued diffidently, "But it can also be a little frightening to have someone like that so single-mindedly in love with one . . . there is a feeling of being possessed, of having so much to live up to!" She caught her breath on a rueful self-denigrating laugh. "Am I making any kind of sense?"

"Well, it certainly sounds a very uncomfortable state to be in," Perdita agreed, finding it difficult to contemplate ever being in such a situation—particularly with regard to Lord St. Ive!

"Yes, it was. And then Harry came along, you see, and he was so different! He made me feel loved and cherished . . . and so *safe*! Mama was furious, of course, but Lord St. Ive really behaved quite well when one considers the blow to his esteem. He said that he would not have me made miserable on any account . . . a-and withdrew his suit." Amaryllis stared blankly at the square of lace-edged cambric which she had been slowly mangling into ribbons, and then up at Perdita. "I have not seen him from that day until this week when he called upon us right out of the blue. . . ." She gave Perdita a brief account of what had occurred. "So you can quite see why Harry is so hurt."

"I can see that he might want to knock St. Ive down!" She ignored her friend's fear-filled protestations. "But I'm at a loss to know why he must needs vent his annoyance on you!"

At this point, the door behind them opened and a pleasant sandy-haired young man entered the room and stood irresolute, not immediately recognizing Perdita in her blacks. When she turned, however, he hurried forward to envelop her in an affectionate hug.

"I say, this is a surprise! I had no idea! How are you bearing up? You had our letter, of course?"

She smiled at the spontaneity of his welcome. "Thank you, yes. It has been enormous help to me to have the loving support of friends; and you were at the funeral, too, Mr. Windlesham told me. That was good of you. I was only sorry you couldn't come to the house afterward."

"So was I. I regarded Sir Edwin almost in the light of an uncle or some such, as you well know. Unfortunately I had a prior commitment."

The preliminaries over, an uncomfortable silence fell, and Perdita saw that Harry's good-natured features wore an unaccustomed look of strain. He felt her glance come to rest on him and then move to mark the telltale traces of tears on his wife's face, and his fair sensitive skin grew a trifle pink. An uncomfortable sense of guilt aroused his belligerence, and Amaryllis's delightful lower lip began to tremble once more.

"Oh heavens!" cried Perdita, nobly resisting the temptation to box both pairs of ears. "My dears, this really will not do! Harry, you should be ashamed of yourself. You have a wife in a thousand, but if you're such a slowtop as to give any credence to Miss Prothero's poisonous little barbs, I don't think you deserve to keep her!"

"Well, of course I don't believe that woman! Lord, Perdita, what *do* you take me for? Dearest Amaryllis, is that what you have been thinking?" He held out his arms, and with a sob Amaryllis flew into them. "Oh, my poor love, as if I would ever doubt you! It was hearing everyone talking about you and that fellow! He has such address! I was stupidly jealous, I admit it!"

Watching them kissing and cuddling, each assuring the other that it had been the greatest misunderstanding ever, and that it would never happen again, Perdita began to feel distinctly *de trop*. People in love behaved so strangely that she seriously doubted if she would ever understand, and as to finding herself in a similar situation ... with a curious pang of regret she had to admit that such a possibility was highly unlikely.

Eventually she said dryly, "I have no wish to throw a damper on this joyful reconciliation, my dears, but I must go. Midge will have been sitting in the Pump Room this hour or more, wondering where I have got to."

Amaryllis nobly insisted that Harry must walk back with her, and because Perdita wanted a private word with him, she accepted.

"You must be wishing me at the devil," she said as they walked. "Dragging you from your wife at such a moment."

The vehemence of his denial lacked credibility, and meeting her amused glance, he grinned. "Oh well, a little waiting never hurt—besides, least I could do. Very grateful, m'dear, for showing me the error of my ways. Stupid thing, pride and all that!"

Perdita dismissed her part in the matter with a rather preoccupied air. "Harry—what are you going to do about St. Ive?"

"Do about him?" Harry echoed with a frown. "I know what I'd like to do about him!"

"No, that wouldn't answer," she said quickly. "It would simply provide further fuel for gossip. But if his lordship elects to remain any length of time at Anderley, as well he might, there is every likelihood that sooner or later your paths will cross."

"Well, he'd better keep his distance if he don't want me to plant him a facer!"

"Oh, Harry, do try to be sensible!" Much as it

went against the grain with her to in any way rescue Lord St. Ive from his own folly, Perdita felt obliged to say, "You had much better meet him in as friendly a manner as you can muster and in as public a place as possible." She saw his chin begin to jut and added firmly, "For Amaryllis's sake!"

It was this last appeal as much as anything which won the day, Harry being struck afresh by the necessity of protecting his beloved from vulgar tattle. "Well, I daresay I can bring myself to be civil to his lordship," he said magnanimously, as they crossed Pulteney Bridge and approached the Pump Room. "We did get along quite tolerably at the first, after all."

"Splendid," said Perdita. "And I daresay you will not have to suffer him for too long, for the London Season will soon be in full swing and I cannot see him willingly forgoing its pleasures, so unless you mean to take Amaryllis to London, you may soon be easy."

Harry was called upon to make good his word rather sooner than he had expected due solely to his insistence upon staying with Perdita until Miss Midgely was found. It was Perdita who saw the Marquis first. He was standing, head bent a little, the epitome of unstudied elegance, listening to Canon Pennifold's tedious ramblings with so convincing an appearance of patient interest that in other circumstances she might have felt quite charitably disposed toward him. Almost against her will she noticed how, without making the least push to do so, he filled the room with his presence.

And then he looked up. His eyes narrowed, meeting hers, and then moved on to note her companion. He bent to say something close to the elderly clergyman's ear and shook hands with him. Then in the same unhurried way he strolled toward them.

"Harry," she said with a calmness she was far

from feeling, "if you were to meet Lord St. Ive quite out of the blue and offer him your hand, would he respond with any degree of amiability?"

"Lord, Perdita, how should I know? You never can tell with Ivo," he said, dragging his attention away from a particularly handsome lady taking her promenade, whose fashionable like was seldom to be seen in Bath. "Now, I wonder who *she* is?" he mused.

"Harry!"

"What?" He flushed, and grinned with the guilelessness of a child. "Sorry. Just looking! St. Ive, you said. Why do you ask?"

"Because his lordship is this very moment approaching."

"Oh lord!" Harry groaned.

There was a moment when it seemed to Perdita that time stood still, and all her senses were stretched to the limit. She was very much aware of Miss Prothero sitting nearby, her ears very nearly out on stalks, ready to catch the slightest note of discord, and of any number of other interested habitués of the Pump Room equally anxious to speculate and pass judgment.

And then the marquis was standing before them, and preempted the issue by saluting Perdita, his eyes skimming over her with the minimum of recognition, before clapping Harry on the shoulder and drawling in a voice loud enough to be heard by all close to them, "Harry, at last! What an elusive dog you are, to be sure! Did your lovely wife tell you I damn near ran off with her the other day? Well, as far as Mrs. Windlesham's, anyway. Amaryllis isn't with you?"

Harry found himself responding in similar vein almost without effort, and in a trice they were all sitting around a table, and her companions were conversing in a way that rendered Perdita speechless as much from shock as from being deliberately excluded. What two-faced creatures men were, she decided indignantly, listening to them exchanging news of mutual friends in the most commonplace way ever, for all the world as though they had never been rivals for Amaryllis's hand!

She was roused from these wrathful observations by his lordship's saying in quite a different tone, so low that only she and Harry could hear, "Well, that should give the tabbies food for thought, wouldn't you say?"

Perdita half turned to him, surprised. "Then you knew . . . you were aware of what was being said?"

His eyes were expressionless beneath their lazy lids. "My dear Miss Grant, only a totally insensitive blockhead could have remained in ignorance of it, and though I am many things, I hope I am not that!" He dared her to contradict him, and when she remained silent, he continued ironically, "I had no idea I should find Bath such a breeding ground of intrigue!" He turned to Harry. "I am only sorry that, by my carelessness, I have caused Amaryllis embarrassment. Pray give her my apologies and assure her that I would never knowingly harm her."

The mood did not last, however, for his next words contained a distinct note of censure.

"It would seem, Harry, that you take the whole thing considerably more lightly, or does your appearance here with Miss Grant signify some brilliant stroke of strategy which has me confounded?"

Harry's brows drew together ominously, and Perdita, containing her own fury, broke in swiftly, "Oh, Harry and I have known each other forever. We practically grew up in each other's pockets. You can be sure no one here will find anything remarkable in our being together."

"Indeed?"

Feeling that Harry was about to say something cutting, she continued hastily, "You must find Bath tediously slow by comparison with London, my lord. I daresay you will be wishing to return there with all possible speed?"

He fingered the riband of his quizzing glass and smiled, but it was a smile quite without that warmth of a moment ago. In fact, she was obliged to suppress an instinctive urge to shiver.

"Sometimes, Miss Grant," he said, "one must put duty before mere self-gratification. I shall not leave Anderley until I am satisfied that my father is past all danger!"

MISS MIDGELY FOUND Perdita unusually quiet in the carriage on the way home. She put it down to the strain of mingling with so many people and being obliged to endure much reminiscence about Sir Edwin.

"I must say, I was pleasantly surprised by the Duke of Anderley's son," she ventured by way of trying to draw Perdita out of her introspection. "Such elegant manners. Mrs. Windlesham introduced him to me. He seems quite touchingly concerned about his father."

Something remarkably like a snort of derision greeted this observation, so that Almeria Midgely looked more closely at her companion. Two bright spots of color stood out on Perdita's cheeks. "Are you all right, my dear?"

"Perfectly!" came the clipped reply.

"Well, you don't look quite yourself. I shouldn't wonder if you haven't overdone things a little."

"Oh, of all the idiotish notions!" Perdita stopped, drew a deep steadying breath, and concluded lightly, "Sorry, Midge. You are quite right, as always. I have been more than usually busy, and have ended up insufferably blue-deviled. But that is no reason for taking it out on you!"

There was a hint of something in her voice that made Miss Midgely curious as to what exactly she had been up to, but she sensed that now was not the moment to press for answers.

When they presently arrived home, it was to encounter a small hired chaise pulling out of the driveway and turned in the direction of Bath.

"Whatever . . . ?" Perdita urged Silas to make haste. "We aren't expecting anyone, are we, Midge?"

"That's one of the rigs from the White Hart, ma'am," the coachman offered. "I recognized the boy driving."

Perdita sprang down as soon as the carriage stopped and ran up the steps, leaving Midge to follow at a more decorous pace. In the hall surrounded by a quantity of baggage stood a vision in primrose-colored pantaloons and a coat extravagantly cut and nipped in at the waist.

"Good God!" she exclaimed faintly. "Bertram!"

Chapter 6

*I*T WAS SOME MOMENTS before Perdita could collect her wits enough to take in the full import of Bertram's presence there in the hall. Indeed, it was the arrival of Miss Midgely, as curious in her own way as Perdita to know who had come visiting, who broke the spell.

"Gracious!" she exclaimed, and then, seeing the butler hovering uncertainly in the background, pulled herself together. 'Tea," she said briskly. "At once, Fletcher, if you please, in the drawing room." And in the manner of the schoolroom she bustled them both upstairs.

"But you can't possibly stay here, Bertram!" Perdita insisted for the umpteenth time as the argument flowed back and forth over the teacups.

"I don't see why not, cousin." There was a faint stubborn whine to his voice. "I always did when Uncle Edwin was alive. Nearest thing to a home I had latterly."

"Yes, well, Grandpa isn't here now," she said, refusing to be swayed by false sentiment. "And it is hardly two weeks since you swept out in high dudgeon, swearing terrible oaths against him and vowing never to set foot over the threshold again!

Not to mention the little matter of the letter you wrote me."

"Yes, well, you can't blame me for that! That cursed will! But I've had time to think now, and I quite see that I was overhasty, laying the blame at your door—I mean, dammit, we should be drawing closer, not quarreling!"

"Why?"

He stared at her blankly, saw only polite interest in her face, and swallowed nervously. "Because— because of our relationship! We have neither of us another soul in the world but each other!"

"Oh, I see. And that concerns you, does it?"

"Well, naturally." He rose and began to pace about nervously. "I mean, I can see now that it was wholly selfish of me, walking out like that! Families should stick together at times like this. And you, cousin—a woman on her own needs a man to care for her, protect her." Why did he have the growing feeling that he was being played like a fish? He stumbled on, "To—to lend her support—"

"To spend her money?" she concluded softly.

"No! No, of course not." Bertram ran a finger under the outrageously high points of his collar, wishing Perdita did not keep the room so deucedly hot.

"Oh, cut line, Bertie!" Perdita exclaimed in sudden exasperation. "This is me, remember? I'm more than five, and can read you through and through! I always could. At a guess, I'd say that you have discovered the will can't be overset, your pockets are all to let, and you've come to try to borrow money."

"You know, Perdita," he retorted peevishly, "you've got a cursed unfeeling way with you sometimes! It's no small wonder to me that you've never married—a man don't like being made to feel small, I can tell you! As a matter of fact, that's why I came. M-marriage, I mean. I know you didn't take to the idea before, but that was the old man's doing, and circumstances have changed now. A woman on her own, as I said, needs a man—a husband, in fact—"

Her peal of laughter stopped him in midflow. "Oh, Bertram! You do try, I'll give you that! But I didn't expect even you to come about so quickly. You must indeed be in desperate straits!"

Sadly, the very streak of vanity in Bertram Tillot that most invited ridicule also prohibited him from appreciating the absurdity of his behavior. His florid features became flushed and contorted with chagrin; Perdita's mirth seemed to be mocking him, and that Midgely woman didn't help—sitting in the background, impassively plying her needle and watching him, for all the world like one of those deuced old crones that were supposed to cluster around the guillotine watching while the Froggie heads rolled. He flung himself into a chair and moodily surveyed his shining Hessians extended before him in all their glory. Life, he concluded, could be very unfair.

Perdita nibbled her lip ruefully. Little as she sympathized with Bertram's weakness of character, it had not been her intention to make fun of him, and it had not needed the brief reproving glance from Midge to prompt her now to tell him so in her usual impulsive fashion. But he cut her short with a brittle mirthless laugh.

"Oh, don't trouble to apologize! With your usual acuteness you have seen through me. I never could pull wool with you, could I? The fact is," he said jerkily, "I'm all to pieces—gutted! I'm being dunned right and left, and I haven't so much as a sixpence to scratch with!"

Perdita's heart sank. "You don't precisely look like a pauper," she said, regarding his dandified appearance with deep suspicion. "Furthermore, I wouldn't have thought a man in such dire straits as you describe could run to a valet."

He looked huffy. "A man must still dress. And anyway, Bridge has elected to remain with me, foolishly no doubt in your opinion, though I ain't paid him a groat in ages."

"I had no idea you could inspire such loyalty," she said lightly, and then, sobering, "How much do you owe?"

"Oh, Lord knows." He hazarded a sum that dismayed her.

"But how could you possibly have run up such an amount? I know for a fact that Grandpa cleared your outstanding debts not six months since."

"You don't suppose I told him the whole, do you? He'd have washed his hands of me there and then if I had!"

"And you think I won't?" she retorted angrily.

"Not if you'll just listen for a minute instead of flying up into the boughs!" He sat forward with renewed eagerness. "The thing is, you'd find me the most accommodating of husbands if we were to marry—I wouldn't expect you to be forever hanging on my arm, and only consider the benefits. I would be able to pay the most pressing of the gull-gropers and duns, and the rest would be happy to wait. Wouldn't care to offend me, d'you see, knowing that I was a man of substance."

"I see all too clearly," she said with an irony that escaped him. "What is less clear, however, is what the advantages are to be for me in this admirable arrangement."

"Well, I thought *that* would be as plain as your nose!" he said ingenuously. "I mean, just being a married lady, for a start. You'd have a deal more freedom, and besides, it stands to reason that whatever expectations you might hope to entertain, the simple fact is that the more time goes on, the less likely you are to receive anything like an eligible offer."

"At my advanced age, you mean?" she queried with deceptive meekness.

"Not just that," he said magnanimously. "But Bath ain't exactly spilling over with eligible bachelors! Dull as ditchwater, most of 'em, or in their dotage. You'd much better have me, coz—I wouldn't interfere, you'd be able to do exactly as you please."

"But I can do that now," she said, tiring suddenly of his intolerable conceit. "And without being reduced to penury by an improvident mate. Thank you, Bertie, but I must refuse your gallant offer. I am not yet *that* desperate to marry!"

There was so much fire and resolution in her voice that he knew further persuasion would be less than useless. He sprang to his feet.

"No! I'm not good enough for you, am I? You've got your line cast and running for plumper fish! Oh, don't think I haven't twigged your game, but he's too slippery by far to take the lure, and you're like to end up looking very foolish, let me tell you! You a duchess, egad! It's enough to make the cat laugh!"

Perdita had also risen, her patience with him quite at an end, but inwardly dismayed to discover that he, too, had somehow misinterpreted her relationship with the duke. Surely she had done nothing to encourage such a notion? She put the thought from her and faced Bertram, her voice cold.

"I don't know what particular maggot you've got in your brain, Bertie, but I've no wish to listen to your ravings, so if you have quite finished, I think you had better leave before we both say more than we ought."

Her words seemed to freeze him into immobility. "B-but you can't turn me away. I haven't anywhere to go! The landlord's repossessed my rooms, and I've been punting on tick for so long now that there's hardly anywhere I dare show my face in town anymore!"

"You should have thought of that—"

"Dammit, don't preach at me!" he exploded, his voice grown shrill with the onset of fear. "Look, Perdita," he pleaded. "If you won't marry me, at least help me! Just two or three thousand—you wouldn't miss it. Uncle Edwin left you more than ten times as much! And it would make all the difference to me."

In spite of all her resolve, Perdita could feel herself being moved by his plight. She looked helplessly toward Midge and received a disapproving shake of the head accompanied by a silently mouthed "no."

"I can't see that it would answer, even if I agreed," she said, trying to remain firm. "Besides, we both know what you would do with it."

"I wouldn't, I swear! I'd be able to spread enough of it around the more pressing of my creditors to keep them sweet, *and* I'd pay the landlord—and still keep enough for one decent stake—"

"Oh, for heaven's sake!" cried Perdita.

"No, it'll be all right! Look, it's not easy to explain, coz, but a fellow gets a kind of feeling when his luck's on the turn—"

"Perhaps he does," she cut in. "But only a fool persistently gambles beyond his means. And do stop calling me *coz* in that irritating way. If it's some curious attempt to play on our relationship in the hope of persuading me to send good money after bad, you are quite out!"

"You sound just like the old man!" he sneered, his eyes wild, his color now alarmingly high. "God, I should have known he'd poison your mind against me!"

"Nothing so melodramatic, I assure you, though I should indeed be going against everything he expected of me if I allowed you to sway me." She tried to sound firm. "But the plain fact is, I know what you are, and I cannot think it would be right for me to encourage you in your folly. And that is that."

Her words at last seemed to silence him, but as he stood staring at her, his whole aspect filled her with alarm. He looked like a man teetering on the edge of an abyss who suddenly knows what his fate must be. At last, blindly, he groped his way to the chair beside the window table and sat down, burying his head in his hands. "Then I'm finished!" he groaned.

For once Perdita felt that he was not play-acting, and his distress moved her more than she would have thought possible. She looked again at Midge, who raised her eyebrows expressively. She sighed resignedly.

"All right, Bertie," she said. "You can stay here for a few days—a few days only," she repeated as his head came up with remarkable alacrity. "And we'll see what can be worked out."

"Undoubtedly I am a fool," she said to Midge when Bertram had left the room with a faintly disapproving Fletcher.

"You are," agreed Almeria Midgely with dour certainty. "That young man will be a millstone around your neck forever if you don't take a firm stand now."

IT WAS AN OPINION shared by the duke when Perdita next called on him. He gave her one of his heavy-lidded stares.

"Strange," he mused. "Until now I have always taken you for a young woman of sense."

"I know," she said with a rueful shrug. "I suppose it was guilt, partly. I couldn't help feeling that Grandpa had treated Bertram a bit shabbily in his will. And he really was desperate—it wasn't a sham."

"A dangerous emotion, guilt. It can lead one into all kinds of unwise decisions. I don't know young Tillot, but I know the type. The obsessive gambler will use every device from low cunning to out-and-out treachery to fund his habit."

Perdita was beginning to feel pressured—first Midge, and now the duke. "I promise you I know what I'm about," she said stiffly. She met his eyes and bit her lip, half smiling. "Truly. I have no intention of squandering Grandpa's money on Bertram." In an attempt to change the subject, she asked casually, "Is your son still with you?"

"He is, much to my surprise. I confess I had expected him to lose interest within a couple of days, but there is no mention of his going. In fact—the duke's voice was unusually gruff—"he talks of bringing some quack down from London—a crony of Gentleman Jackson, who is something of a miracle-worker with injuries such as mine. Not," he added caustically, "that I have any time for that kind of moonshine!"

"Oh, but it is surely worth a try!" Perdita exclaimed, feeling for the moment quite charitably disposed toward the marquis. "I know how trying you must find it to be so confined."

"We shall see," was all he would say. "Meanwhile as we await the fellow's arrival Piers seems content to pass his time shooting rabbits, or visiting Bath. But he must find life damnably dull, so I doubt he'll stick at either for long."

Perdita, uncomfortably aware that the marquis might have more than one motive for remaining at Anderley, wondered whether she ought to find some way of broaching the subject, but it seemed impossible to do so without sounding vulgarly encroaching or totally bizarre.

"I think, perhaps," she said at last, trying to appear offhand, "that I might come less often to see you now that you are so much improved, and have your son to bear you company."

The sound of water splashing into the fountain was the only thing to disturb the stillness. Then: "As you will," he said with pronounced hauteur. "You have had your fill of elderly invalids, I daresay. To be continuing to give up your time in such a way must inevitably pall."

"Oh no! That isn't the reason at all! I very much enjoy coming to visit you."

"Well then?"

Perdita knew him well enough by now to know that he would not be fobbed off with tame excuses. She became very busy with her gloves, arranging them on her knee and smoothing the creases from them as she sought the right words. Finally, without looking up, she managed a halting explanation.

"It has recently been brought to my attention that my frequent visits here might be open to . . . misinterpretation."

She wasn't sure what she had expected—some kind of explosive reaction, certainly. But in the event the duke was silent for so long that she at last ventured to lift her head, and found him regarding her in a highly quizzical way.

"I am flattered," he drawled. "Would that I might be more deserving of such speculation! Were I but thirty years younger, now . . ." His eyes glinted wickedly, affording her a disturbing glimpse of how irresistible that younger Anderley must have been. He seemed not displeased by her ensuing confusion. "Does it trouble you to find your name linked with mine?"

"For myself, no," Perdita protested, collecting

her errant thoughts. "I have never given a straw for what anyone might say of me."

"Wise child," he mocked gently. "Well, you certainly need not be protective of *my* good name, since I never had one to speak of! But I confess I'd give a monkey to know who laid the poison. That oaf of a clergyman, was it? Sounds just like the narrow-minded claptrap one might expect from him!"

She hastened to assure him that it wasn't Mr. Gilles, and wished fervently that she had never been lured into what was like to become a tortuous progression of evasions should his grace decide to pursue his interrogation. Thankfully, however, he seemed to be more concerned with her state of mind.

"You don't seem overly reassured, my young friend. Why is that, I wonder?"

Unable to sit still any longer, Perdita rose and took a few steps away from him before swinging around to face him. "For one thing," she began, "I wouldn't want *you* to suppose that I may have done . . . anything I have done, out of motives other than . . ."

"Charity?" he suggested dryly.

"Friendship," she was swift to correct him.

"Agreed. And so?" he pressed her to continue. "You said *for one thing*—so what other bees do you have buzzing around in that lovely head?"

She flung away to stare out of the window, and was in time to see the marquis striding along the terrace, a shotgun cradled across his arm. "I'm not sure," she said in a stifled voice, "whether I can continue to come here as I have done in the past without embarrassment . . . a loss of that easy comradeship . . ."

The duke followed the direction of her glance with some curiosity, and a great many unanswered questions suddenly became clear. "Ah," he said softly. "I begin to understand." And, viewing her betraying blush with interest, "Naturally, I have no wish to embarrass you, my dear. If you decide to curtail your visits, I shall not take offense, though it does seem a pity, when your state of mourning must of necessity restrict your activities, that you should be deprived of one of your few remaining pleasures. However . . ."

Something in his voice at this point engaged her full attention.

"You might care to consider the alternative I am about to offer you. My dear Perdita, how would you fancy a little sport? The opportunity to turn the tables on our accuser and give him something to feed his suspicions?"

Chapter 7

THE OUTRAGEOUSNESS of the duke's suggestion occupied perdita's thoughts to the exclusion of all else as she made her way home.

"I couldn't possibly!" had been her immediate reaction.

"Why not?" he had countered. "Only consider how splendidly a trifling degree of verbal dalliance would serve to alleviate the tedium of our respective lives—and in so doing, teach a certain impudent young dog a lesson."

"It would be quite iniquitous!" But already her eyes had begun to sparkle. "Only consider his lordship's fury when he discovers the truth, as he must in time."

"You may safely leave my son to me, child," said the duke in a voice that made her glad she would not be in the marquis's shoes when that time came. "And no blame will attach to you. You have my word on't. So, what do you say?"

And, God forgive her, she had said yes. Why, she was still not sure. If it was simply to spite St. Ive, she would be well served if he vented his fury upon her later, for notwithstanding the duke's assurances, she had little doubt that he would find a way to get back at her. Perhaps it was the element of danger that had spurred her on? A powerful antidote to boredom, of which she was likely to have a surfeit in the next few months.

As she walked from the stable through the gardens toward the house, she scarcely heard the garden boy's greeting, and the burgeoning flower beds went unnoticed. Only as she ascended the steps to the side door did a shout penetrate her abstraction. Bertram's voice—and at the same moment a scraping, rushing sound.

She hesitated, half turned in the direction of Bertram's voice just as a shower of dust and small stones engulfed her and something heavy, missing her head by no more than a fraction of an inch, caught her a glancing blow on the shoulder and sent her sprawling across the flagstones.

"My God! Perdita—are you all right?"

More winded than hurt, she brushed the dust from her eyes in time to see Bertram, his pose of indolent perfection abandoned, sprinting across the garden toward her, his face unbecomingly reddened and distorted with alarm. Without a thought for his yellow calf-clingers he dropped on his knees beside her.

"Pray, do not try to move!" he besought her as she struggled into a sitting position. "Here, you!" he called to the garden boy, who had by now joined them. "Go indoors at once—find Fletcher and tell him what has happened!"

The boy was up the steps and gone before Perdita could stop him. "I'm all right, Bertie—don't fuss, I beg of you!" she muttered, while her fingers gingerly explored the rent in her dress where she had been struck. "What was it, for heaven's sake?"

When he did not immediately answer, she eased her painful neck muscles and slowly turned her head to find Bertram staring wordlessly at an urn-shaped object, all of twelve inches in length and made of solid stone, one side of which had shattered where it hit the ground. He stepped back, shielding his eyes from the sun.

"It's part of the pediment," he said tersely. "The whole of one end has come down!"

Before she could comment, the boy was back with Fletcher hurrying in his wake, and followed moments later by cook. A certain amount of pandemonium ensued during which Perdita, wiping a disagreeable quantity of grit from her mouth, informed them all that she was not in need of being carried, and that if someone would but help her to her feet, she could quite well manage to make her way indoors—and the garden boy, in the enviable position of having witnessed the whole incident, announced to all who might care to listen that in his opinion, it was only the gentleman's shouting a warning to Miss Perdita that had saved her from being killed entirely.

In a very short space of time she was being helped up the stairs, to be met at the top by Miss Midgely, who had been discreetly informed by Fletcher of what had happened.

"I think, my dear, you should go and lie down," Almeria Midgely said without fuss, adding in a quiet tone, "Mrs. Windlesham is in the drawing room, and I think we might only distress her if she were to see you with your dress all torn."

Perdita, feeling more shaken than she would admit, her legs trembling from climbing the stairs, threw her a look of gratitude. But before she could proceed, the door to the drawing room was pulled open and Mrs. Windlesham's bulk filled the opening.

"Is something amiss? I would not think of staying if . . . Oh, my goodness gracious! Perdita, my dear . . . whatever has befallen you? Miss Midgely, you

must send for Dr. Bryant directly! Oh, you poor
child . . ."

For Perdita it was just one irritation too many.
She really did not feel at all the thing, and the
booming of Mrs. Windlesham's voice seemed to
echo and grow in her head. As she watched with a
kind of fascination the mouth opening and shut-
ting without pause, the noise seemed to go far
away, and with a strangled sound that was half
laugh, half sob, she sank to the floor in a dead
faint.

"WELL, OF COURSE," said Dr. Byrant, "if you will be
so foolish as to seek to demonstrate your superior-
ity over other mortals by insisting upon behaving
as though nothing had happened, you must take
the consequences."

"I just didn't want any fuss," she said with unaccustomed meekness.

She was lying in her own bed, between cool
sheets, her shoulder bound up and already feeling
more comfortable. And her head ached.

"Although you were not aware of it, the falling
masonry must have just skimmed your head," the
doctor explained. "There is a graze running below
the temple and into your hairline." He eyed her
with severity. "You are a very lucky young woman.
An inch or so nearer and you wouldn't be here
now. As it is, there are no bones broken, though
you'll not be using that arm for a while." He took a
bottle from his bag and poured a small quantity of
liquid into a glass. "That will help the aches and
pains."

"But I won't have to stay in bed?"

His thickly sprouting black eyebrows described
a wild arch. "If I thought there was the remotest
chance of being attended to, I'd say you should
stay there for at least forty-eight hours. As it is . . ."

He turned resignedly to Miss Midgely. "Try to keep her there for the rest of today, and as much of tomorrow as you can manage. I'll be in to see her in a day or so."

But in the event, Miss Midgely's powers of persuasion were not put to the test. Perdita slept fitfully, waking only for drinks—and once, Bertram was permitted to see her briefly.

"How are you feeling?"

"Rather strange." She managed a weak smile. "Dr. Bryant's draft must have been more potent than I thought." Her eyelids were already beginning to droop again, but she held sleep at bay for long enough to say drowsily, "I believe that I owe you my life, Bertie. 'Thank you' seems a little inadequate—"

"And quite unnecessary, coz," he demurred with charming modesty. "It all happened so quickly that I cannot in conscience take credit." But his disarming self-effacement was wasted, for she was already asleep.

By morning she was feeling much more herself, and though her shoulder ached and her head still nursed a faint but persistent throb, she announced her intention of getting up later in the day. Long before then, however, Mollie had come staggering up to her bedchamber almost hidden under the biggest basket of flowers Perdita had ever seen.

"Goodness!"

"Aren't they the prettiest blooms you ever did see, ma'am?" gasped the little maid, grown uncharacteristically loquacious in the face of such extravagance. "Every kind you could think of! And there's an even bigger basket downstairs in the drawing room. From his grace's hothouses," she concluded in hushed awe, touching a finger to a particularly exquisite long-stemmed red rose.

A note came with the flowers, expressing his

grace's distress upon hearing from Mrs. Windlesham of her accident. Perdita groaned inwardly. Doubtless the whole district would by now have been apprised of what had happened, and the details would not have grown less in the telling! The truth of this was borne out as throughout the morning the doorbell seemed never to be still, the well-wisher ranging from Mr. Gilles, who had expressed his deep shock and avowed his intention of calling again just as soon as Miss Grant should feel well enough to receive him, to a child from one of the families in the village whom Perdita visited regularly, who brought a simple posy of wild flowers.

Bertram, exploiting his role as hero of the hour, had borrowed funds from a grateful Perdita and had taken himself off to Bath. The house was momentarily peaceful, and by midafternoon, not withstanding Midge's long face, Perdita had made the transition from her bed to the sofa in the drawing room. Here everything had been arranged for her comfort, and a cashmere shawl was tucked lovingly around her though a huge fire roared merrily up the chimney as though it were December instead of early May.

"There's no sense taking chances, Miss Perdita," said Mary, the most senior of the household servants apart from Fletcher, as she gave the shawl a final tweak. "It's when we're at our lowest ebb that chills and the like strike us down. That's what my ma always told us, and whose to say she's wrong, beggin' your pardon, miss."

"I certainly wouldn't dream of doing so." Perdita smiled. "Thank you, Mary. I am being shockingly spoiled."

She would have preferred to dress, but with her right arm bound across her chest to prevent any aggravation of the shoulder injury, she was obliged to admit defeat and settle instead for a dressing gown, the most comfortable of which proved also to be the most frivolous, being a loose robe of floating oyster-gray silk which covered the injured arm with ease and closed at the neck with layers of ruffles.

"I look like your pupil again," she had teased Midge as her hair was gently brushed and looped back with a ribbon so as not to hurt her grazed head.

Miss Midgely frowned. "If you were, I might have more control over you."

Perdita did not admit even to herself, let alone to Midge, how tiresomely weak she felt after taking those few steps down to the drawing room; how wayward her legs seemed to have become in the face of so slight an effort, for all the world as though the bones had been removed from them. But once settled on the sofa she soon recovered. The warmth of the fire induced a not unpleasant languor, so that Midge had not read more than two pages of *Guy Mannering* to her before her eyelids began to droop. Almeria Midgely nodded with quiet satisfaction and closed the book. She drew her tapestry frame toward her and was deeply engrossed with her needle when the doorbell pealed distantly below. A few moments later Fletcher came softly in.

The first thing Perdita heard was Fletcher apparently announcing the Marquis of St. Ive. "Oh no, I can't possibly see him!" she cried, struggling out of her somewhat inelegant slump among the cushions and gasping involuntarily as pain seemed to run through every part of her.

"There now," Miss Midgely reproved, laying aside her work and moving unhurriedly to help her into a more comfortable position and rearrange the cushions accordingly. "Is that better? Naturally Lord St. Ive does not expect you to receive him. He is, however, charged with the obligation of taking back to his grace a comprehensive report of your injury and progress, which I am this minute going down to convey to him."

"No—wait," Perdita said, having collected her scattered wits. "I assume Lord St. Ive is in the book room, Fletcher?"

"That's right, Miss Perdita. I took the liberty of offering his lordship a glass of Madeira before I brought his card upstairs."

She nodded approval. St. Ive would not be able to complain of shabby treatment at her hands. "Then perhaps you will ask him to be so good as to step up here for a moment?" In vain Miss Midgely protested. Perdita remained adamant. "Don't fuss, Midge—five minutes' conversation will hardly kill me. You see, I know the duke. He won't easily be satisfied with hearsay. Much better if his lordship can reassure him that he has seen me looking far from prostrate and at death's door!"

St. Ive was not altogether pleased to find himself asked upstairs; he had come in the first place only to prevent his father from so doing, having returned from a morning ride to find him on the point of being carried out to his carriage. Nothing short of positive assurances on his part that he would bring back chapter and verse of what exactly had befallen Miss Grant, following upon Mrs. Windlesham's somewhat emotional account of falling masonry and deathlike faints, would suffice to calm his agitation of spirit. Such behavior was so alien to anything St. Ive knew of his father that he found it profoundly disturbing. For the first time he was obliged to face that fact that the duke had indeed become infatuated with Miss Grant. He refused to grace it with the name of love.

Fletcher eyed the austere profile with some diffidence as he presently showed his magnificent visitor the way. "Beg pardon, my lord," he ventured, "but Miss Midgely would be grateful if you was not to stay above a minute or so. Only Miss Perdita shouldn't be out of bed by rights, let alone be receiving."

St. Ive lifted an ironical eyebrow. "Got a will of her own, has she?"

To his surprise, the butler chuckled quietly. "Sir Edwin raised her to know what's what, and that's a fact, my lord," he said with the familiarity of an old family retainer. "But a better, kinder mistress I couldn't wish for."

"Indeed?" St. Ive, unused to conversing with servants, felt that some reply, however brief, was required, and was rewarded with an unsolicited account of Miss Grant's history—how she had been orphaned when little more than a baby, the only child of Sir Edwin's only son, and had been brought up by Sir Edwin from that time on. "Fair doted on Miss Perdita, he did, my lord—but he had his own way of doing things—no mamby-pambying nonsense, as he termed it, for her . . ." There was pride mingled with very real distress at the loss of his master in the elderly butler's voice, but St. Ive was relieved when they at last reached the door of the drawing room, where Fletcher announced him with the ceremony he considered due to the occasion.

His first impression as politenesses were exchanged was of warmth—not mere physical warmth, which indeed there was, but rather a general air of comfort and good taste without pretentious formality. His second, almost simultaneous sensation was an acute awareness of the figure on the sofa near the fire, even a sense of shock occasioned by the change in Miss Grant's appearance. As she lay back among her cushions, there seemed to be an aura of frailty, of angelic vulnerability about her that was quite at odds with his normal expectation of her. It crossed his mind involuntarily that she might have contrived just such an impression for his benefit—had chosen that gray frothy confection of a gown deliberately to enhance the deep shadows beneath her eyes.

He might have continued to think so had she not sat forward with determined brightness to greet him, extending her left hand a trifle awkwardly as she invited him to take a seat, for in so doing he was made acutely aware of the way the gown was drawn across her right side, the imperfectly concealed wince of pain—and although the eyes that met his lacked none of their directness, he glimpsed in their depths the echo of that pain. It made him speak more gently than he would otherwise have done.

"I am sorry about your accident. I trust you are not suffering too much discomfort?"

"Thank you, no," she answered with a flagrant disregard for the truth. "I shall do very well presently. I am bruised, but nothing is broken."

St. Ive noted the two spots of color high on her cheekbones that he suspected owed rather more to fever than the heat of the fire, and wondered. But it was Miss Midgely who voiced his doubts, saying bluntly that Perdita would do a great deal better if she heeded Dr. Bryant's advice, and received an impatient shrug for her pains.

"Well, I shall not stay to tire you, ma'am," he said. "I do but come to set my father's mind at rest. The account he received of what happened was so alarming as to fill him with a very real anxiety for your health."

"Mrs. Windlesham is a dear, but her capacity for exaggeration is, I fear, notorious," Perdita said lightly, "and in this case, as you can see, my lord, is typically wide of the mark." She explained briefly what had happened. "And that was all—it was but a small section of the pediment that broke away—"

"It was a piece of solid stone twice the size of a cannon ball," Almeria Midgely interpolated sharply. "You might well have been killed."

"Yes, well, its size and solidity are irrelevant, since, thanks to my cousin's presence of mind, the damage it caused was negligible, except to my self-esteem, that is!"

The small "Tch" of exasperation that escaped Miss Midgely was not lost on St. Ive. His glance dwelt on the covered injury.

"Your cousin?" he mused. "That will be Mr. Tillot? My father did mention that he was staying with you at present. How fortunate that he was on hand to warn you!"

"Yes, wasn't it? He has gone into Bath this afternoon, or you might have met him." Perdita was beginning to feel vaguely oppressed. In a bid to change the subject she turned her aching head a little stiffly to seek out the duke's extravagant floral tribute. For an instant she had the curious illusion that it was floating in the air. She blinked and said briskly, "Anyhow, you will now be able to reassure his grace that I am making an excellent recovery. And do pray thank him most warmly for his beautiful flowers! I think I have never received anything half so lovely in all my life!"

St. Ive's glance moved also to encompass the flowers, noting the preponderance of red roses among their number. His expression hardened. "He must indeed think a great deal of you."

"Why, so I hope," she returned with deliberate archness, wishing that he would go. The effort of concentrating was making her feel very strange. His face seemed to blur before her eyes, and again she blinked to clear the image. "As you can see," she said, indicating the small jug of wild flowers on the sofa table beside her, "I have more than one admirer. . . ." Her mouth seemed very dry all of a sudden. She ran her tongue around her lips to moisten them. "You will not I hope tell your father that he has a rival. . . ." Her voice faded away, and she put a hand uncertainly to her head.

"Perdita?" It was Midge's voice, sharp with worry, distant at first and then closer . . . and another voice, vaguely familiar . . . then the choking, pungent aroma of smelling salts caught at her throat, making her cough.

There was an arm about her, very gently easing her forward, St. Ive's voice close by. "A drink, ma'am, if you have one handy. Water will do, or cordial—no, not brandy, I think. . . ."

"I'm perfectly all right," Perdita said distinctly as soon as she was able.

"Don't talk, and drink this," said St. Ive, calmly authoritative.

She opened her eyes and found his face poised very close above her, blotting out everything else. Meekly she drank, grateful for the cooling liquid, and afterward he lowered her with infinite care back against the cushions and stood up, glass in hand, staring down at her with a peculiar intensity.

"This is ridiculous," she gasped, attempting flippancy and failing miserably. "I can't think what came over me!"

"Lord St. Ive thinks you may have a touch of concussion," said Midge, with an admirable calmness that brought an approving look from his lordship. "Dr. Bryant did mention it as a possibility, after discovering the cut on your head."

"He didn't mention it to me," she said peevishly, knowing that she was being childish and powerless to stop the weak tears. "It was the m-merest graze!"

"Oh no!" Miss Midgely exclaimed in a distressed

way. "My dear Perdita, don't upset yourself! We will have you back in bed in a trice, and if you will only be patient, I'm sure you will be yourself in no time." She looked apologetically at St. Ive. "Forgive me, my lord. I must see Fletcher to find out what can be managed."

"Yes, of course," he said. "I will take myself out of your way."

"If only that tiresome boy Bertram could be here just once when he was wanted, I might be able to regard him as something less than an encroaching liability!" She drew herself up very straight and looked his lordship in the eyes. "That is cutting up a character, is it not, my lord? Especially when one considers what we owe him. But I *cannot* . . ." She recollected herself, glanced down at Perdita, and shrugged. "Still, that is neither here nor there just at present."

On the point of leaving, St. Ive hesitated. "Do I understand, ma'am, that you have no immediate means of conveying Miss Grant to her room?"

"Well, there is only Fletcher and our garden boy, and neither is precisely suited to the task."

"Then the answer is simple," he said, retracing his steps to the sofa. "If you will direct me where to go, I would be only too happy to oblige."

Perdita roused from her misery to utter distractedly, "No! You can't possibly! I won't permit you to . . ." She glared at him from tear-drowned eyes as he seemed about to swoop on her and lift her high.

"Shut your eyes," he ordered softly, close to her ear, so that Miss Midgely should not hear. "You can always pretend that I am my father!"

"Oh!" But as he lifted her high, she felt too ill to challenge this last provocative jibe, surrendering herself instead to the sure swift competence of his arms. Only as he lowered her gently onto the bed and prepared to leave did she collect herself sufficiently to clutch at him. He turned to look down at her, his face suddenly bleak with hauteur. "Please," she pleaded. "You will not distress your father with . . . any of this?"

The look did not alter, nor was there much comfort in the coldness of his reply. "It would serve no purpose to do so, Miss Grant. Go to sleep now."

Chapter 8

*F*OR THE SECOND TIME in two days Perdita had
suffered the ignominy of being carried to her
bed, and this time there was no swift escape. Dr.
Bryant took his revenge by confining her there for
all of a week, and only when she could convince
him that the last vestige of her headache had vanished was she allowed visitors and the resumption
of a limited regime.

"My dear!" cried Mrs. Windlesham, when permitted to the bedside. "What an ordeal you have
suffered, to be sure! Not that I was in the least
surprised," she added with the complacence of one
who is privy to knowledge not granted to lesser
mortals. "I can't tell you how cast down I was last
week to see you in such a sad way!"

Perdita leaned back against her pillows and allowed the words to flow over her, knowing from
past experience that nothing she could say would
change Mrs. Windlesham's view of things by one
iota.

"And only fancy it being your cousin who saved
you! I said to Mr. Windlesham, 'It only goes to
prove what I have always avowed—that no one is
all bad,' though I am not sure that he was con-

vinced. We have been seeing a great deal of Mr. Tillot in Bath this past week." Mrs. Windlesham leaned forward in her chair to select a sugared plum from the dish offered to her by Perdita, smiling archly as she did so. "I think you may not be aware how very popular you are, my dear Perdita . . . to have saved your life is reckoned to be quite something, I can tell you! No, no, you may blush and protest all you please, but it is so, I promise you!"

The nub of these confidences did little for Perdita's peace of mind. Just contemplating the amount of havoc Bertram could wreak in a week was calculated to bring on a relapse into dizziness—and that she could well do without. A halfhearted attempt to question Bertram himself brought only airy evasions and assurances that she must not be bothering her head about him, "for I have made friends and am having a splendid time!"

I will think about it tomorrow when I am stronger, she promised herself. But one tomorrow drifted into another, and she drifted with them, seemingly incapable of any kind of coherent decision-making.

She still received flowers from the duke almost every day, though the marquis had not attempted to see her since that one embarrassing occasion. Midge told her that he had driven to London very soon afterward and had brought back with him the man who was expected to perform miracles on the duke's ankle. Dr. Bryant was skeptical of his being able to achieve much good, but within a few days of Mr. Septimus Goring's arrival, he owned himself intrigued.

"I'm damned if I know how he does it, but there's some kind of wizardry in the fellow's fingers," he admitted grudgingly. "I had little expectation of his grace's ever walking again. Now, I'm not so sure. I have to admit, I'm impressed."

But Mr. Gilles was less so. "Of course, it is not my place to tell the doctor his business, but the whole enterprise smacks of mumbo-jumbo. The man is obviously a charlatan, and I must say I am astonished that his grace should permit himself to be experimented on in that way!"

"Perhaps," Perdita suggested gently, "when one is in despair, to experiment is all that is left to one?"

"There is such a thing as trusting to the will of God," Mr. Gilles reproved her with a pomposity that put her out of all charity with him.

"Well, I shouldn't tell his grace that if I were you," she advised him crisply. "Furthermore, I doubt the marquis would expose his father to anyone in the least doubtful, for all that there is little love between them."

Her confidence proved to have been justified a few days later. She was walking in the garden with Midge, the weather having turned pleasurably warm, when Mollie came running out of the house in a state of great excitement to tell them that the Duke of Anderley's coach was that very minute bowling up the drive.

"And his grace inside, ma'am, if you please, as large as life—*and* the marquis with him, and Mr. Fletcher was wondering, ma'am, whether it would be in order for him to show the duke, and his lordship, of course, into the book room on account of the stairs perhaps being more than he could manage—"

"Good heavens, child, slow down, do!" exclaimed Miss Midgely. And then, to Perdita, "I had better go in with her to see what is happening. You may follow at your own pace—and don't rush, duke or no duke!"

"No, Miss Midgely," Perdita said with mock

meekness, and grinned. "I believe I will walk around to the front of the house by the path."

When she came in sight of the steps, the coach with its emblem emblazoned on the door was already drawn up and a stockily built gentleman of middle years, resplendent in a black tailcoat, a splendid yellow waistcoat, and a Belcher neckerchief with yellow spots, was superintending the proceedings with an air of unshakable confidence.

"That's the barber," he called encouragingly as two sturdy grooms lowered the Duke of Anderley to the ground in a kind of cut-down sedan chair. That this was accomplished in a dignified manner was in part due to the unfussed air of the self-appointed master of ceremonies, and in part to the duke himself, who looked the epitome of elegance and suffered himself to be thus man-handled with lofty disdain.

Perdita hurried forward as the contraption was set down. "Oh, my dear sir! What a wonderful surprise!"

His eyes gleamed balefully. "Is it not? I am aping Mahomet, you see. Since you have been unable to come to me, I must perforce come to you." He put out a hand, which she grasped eagerly. "You look charming, my dear. You are recovered?" His fingers tightened as he spoke.

"Almost completely," she assured him. "Another day or two and I should have come to you."

"I couldn't wait." His smile was almost boyish. "There is something I would have you witness." He released his hold of her and glanced about him and then at the stranger, who was also giving judicious consideration to the lay of things. "Here will do as well as anywhere, wouldn't you say, Goring?"

"Well enough, your grace. Good level ground and plenty of space."

Perdita's attention was momentarily diverted as, from the corner of her eye, she saw the marquis making a leisurely descent from the coach. Her half-smile was rewarded by a slight inclination of the head accompanied by a chill enigmatic stare. With a quite ridiculous and unexpected feeling of rejection, she turned away, back to his father.

"Come along, man," the duke was exorting one of the grooms. "Step lively with those sticks! Devil take you for a slowtop!" There was a force, a kind of inner excitement about him that found expression in his eyes, reminding Perdita of how he had been when she first knew him, before his accident.

The groom came hurrying across with a pair of stout sticks, and in a very short space of time, with the calm exhortations of the man Goring, to encourage and advise, he was propelling himself forward slowly, with great concentration but with growing confidence, across the ground.

"That will do for now, your grace," said Goring, when he had taken about a dozen painful steps. "We'll not overdo it, if you please. A little at a time, that's the way of it if we're to build up your strength."

Rather to Perdita's surprise, the duke submitted with no more than a grunt and sank back into his improvised chair short of breath but with a triumphant glint of satisfaction.

"But this is wonderful. I couldn't be more pleased!" she exclaimed. "Dr. Bryant told me that you had hopes in time . . . but so soon! You must have worked exceedingly hard!"

"Not I—well, a little, perhaps," confessed his grace with unaccustomed modesty. "Here is the man to whom most of the credit must go." He introduced Mr. Septimus Goring, and Perdita, on closer inspection, found quietness and good humor, and hands that were surprisingly slim, but strong, with long square-ended fingers that gripped hers with firmness.

"I'm pleased to make your acquaintance, ma'am," he said with a courtly bow. "His grace tells me you had a set-to recently with a stone missile and came off badly. Might I venture the opinion that your shoulder is still giving you trouble?"

She stared at him in astonishment and, feeling that everyone was looking at her, including Midge, who had come to the head of the steps, she gave a vexed half-laugh. "There is a trifling stiffness still, but that is only to be expected." Before he could say more she had turned away. "Now you must all come inside and take some refreshment."

This Mr. Goring declined with commendable tact, preferring, he said, if Miss Grant was agreeable, to take a turn in the garden. "Not much of a one for social chit-chat, ma'am." His eyes twinkled. "But if one of your people was to bring me out of a draft of something cooling, now—I'd take it very kindly!"

Later in the book room, as the duke and Miss Midgely conversed together with remarkable amity, Perdita found herself cornered by Lord St. Ive.

"*Does* your shoulder still bother you, Miss Grant?"

His manner was outwardly sanguine, but she mistrusted it. "Dr. Bryant warned me that it would be some time before I lost the stiffness," she said casually. "It was very badly bruised, after all."

"Perhaps you should allow Septimus Goring to take a look at it. He has already worked miracles with my father."

"He has indeed! It has made all the difference in the world to him!" Perdita exclaimed warmly, glancing across to the duke, who was giving Midge his full attention, and heedless, in the wholeheartedness of her appreciation, of the impression that she was creating.

It came as something of a shock, therefore, upon

her turning back to St. Ive, to surprise in him a
look of almost savage anger, so swiftly veiled that
she almost wondered if she had imagined it. Her
lighthearted dismissal of any necessity for such
miracles in her own case trailed away flatly, to be
acknowledged with a polite nod. Unused to finding
the entertainment of a guest so onerous, she felt
her own manner growing agitated, but good manners dictated one last obligation. She hesitated,
and then nerved herself to thank him for what he
had done for her the previous week.

His response was much as she might have expected. "I could hardly ignore your plight, ma'am,"
he drawled, his voice full of silky-soft mockery.
"But don't delude yourself—nothing between us is
changed!"

It was an unequivocal reinforcement of the battle
lines drawn between them. Perdita flushed and bit
her lip.

"I had not supposed otherwise, my lord." She
lifted her chin defiantly. "Pray excuse me. I am
neglecting your father." And she left him, feeling
the shafts of his anger, like little poisoned darts,
penetrating her back as she walked, head high,
across the room.

Miss Midgely had been acquainted with Perdita
for too many years not to recognize a loss of temper when she saw one, however carefully it might
be controlled. Intrigued, she glanced across at his
lordship and found herself suppressing an involuntary shiver. Whatever had Perdita said to him to
warrant such a look?

"Come and sit down, my dear," she said soothingly, relinquishing her chair. "You have been on
your feet quite long enough. And besides, I am
sure his grace would prefer your conversation to
mine." Miss Midgely's eyes twinkled humorously
at him. "I beg you will not trouble to deny it, sir,

for with the greatest respect, I shall not believe you."

The duke chuckled at this departing sally. "An excellent woman you have there, my dear. Remarkably sound."

Perdita resolutely consigned the marquis to perdition and answered with genuine enthusiasm that she didn't know what she would do without Midge. Anderley grunted and sat back, eyeing her critically.

"Well, Perdita," he said at last. "We're a fine pair, are we not?"

"I feel so very foolish," she said wryly. "Coming to grief on my own doorstep!"

"And where is the savior of the hour?" he drawled.

"In Bath, I suspect." It was St. Ive's voice close behind her, making her jump. "Chasing that elusive lady, Luck. Am I not right, Miss Grant?"

"Perdita?" The full awesomeness of the duke's stare fell upon her. "You are never funding that young man's profligacy?"

She immediately flew on to the defensive. "No, of course not! At least . . . he *has* been spending his days in Bath, but it was so very dull for him with me ill. . . ." She forced herself to look up at the marquis. "*Has* he been gambling?"

He lifted an eyebrow. "You surely don't imagine he has been drinking the waters?"

The heavy sarcasm irked her, but she brushed it aside. "No. But he spoke of making friends. . . ." She made a helpless gesture. "I hoped, even though something Mrs. Windlesham said did make me wonder . . . but that is neither here nor there. You see, I knew he had little or no money—"

"From all I hear, that has never hindered him in the past. Besides," St. Ive continued, his drawl an echo of his father's, "he stands at present in the light of a hero—and it would be a brave man who would deny a hero the courtesy of punting on tick!"

"Oh, good God!" she exclaimed, her resentment against him for the moment submerged by a greater annoyance with Bertram.

"My lord, if you know more, I beg you will tell me. If I am to deal with the matter, I must know all."

"No, Perdita," the duke calmly interposed. "This time you will leave the matter to me."

"But you cannot, sir! Oh, forgive me, but it isn't your . . ." She stopped, uncertain how to proceed without sounding impolite.

"It isn't my business," he finished for her imperturbably. "I know it, but I have a fancy to make it mine. You have many excellent qualities, my dear, but you are by far too tender-hearted to see off a basket-scrambler like Tillot." He waved aside her indignant protest. "You might have done so before he made you beholden to him, but now? Come, confess you would find it difficult to send him packing if he don't choose to go."

Perdita's very natural streak of independence wavered before this argument. The prospect of a confrontation with Bertram of the kind she had previously endured, with the added complications of guilt on her side and an ingratiating dismissal of any expectation of gratitude on his part, gave her a sinking feeling. She wavered, and the duke employed his *coup de grace*.

"Also," he said, "it would please me to do this for you."

"You make it very hard for me to refuse," she said hesitantly, and looking up, caught Lord St. Ive's eye. He was at his most sardonic, his look saying as plainly as words, "Don't think I don't know what you're up to, because I do—very well!" It was all she needed to decide her. "And so, dear sir," she concluded warmly, "if you feel up to dealing with my cousin, I shall own myself more than grateful, just so long as you let me know what debts he has incurred. Those I must pay myself."

"Well, we shall see," he said noncommittally.

Not long after the duke and all his entourage had departed, Harry and Amaryllis arrived. They had called the previous week when she was still far from well, and were consequently delighted to see her so much recovered.

"I cannot tell you how distressed we were," Amaryllis confessed, "to see you so . . ."

"Subdued," finished Harry with a grin. "Don't believe I've ever known you so quiet in many a year!"

"Harry!" cried his wife in shocked tones. "Perdita, I beg you will not heed him! He was quite as upset as I, I promise you."

Perdita laughed. "My love, it's all right. I know Harry well enough, I hope, to know when he's funning, and am long past the stage when one falls to weeping at the least slight."

There was much to catch up on in spite of Mrs. Windlesham's wordy accounts of life in Bath. Perdita wanted to know if the gossip about Amaryllis and the marquis had died down, and whether Miss Prothero had found a new victim.

"I must say St. Ive has been most assiduous in his anxiety to quash the rumors," Harry said grudgingly. "Made a point of being seen with both of us as often as possible—he's even taken to visiting the Assembly Rooms, which I doubt he'd deign to do in the ordinary way, and at the dress ball on Monday evening last he was observed by many to be paying marked attention to Grantly's sister, the beautiful one. Stood up twice with her, in fact, and if that don't set the tongues of the gabble-grinders to work, I don't know what will!"

Perdita ought to have felt more pleased than she did, and put it down to tiredness. "Well, I hope he isn't just using Verena Grantly," she said, frowning. "I wouldn't have her hurt any more than you."

"Don't worry, little one," Harry said with a grin. "His lordship may not have tumbled yet, but I suspect that Verena will be the very devil to shift!"

"Dearest," said Amaryllis reproachfully, "I don't like to hear you speaking that way—as if she were some awful scheming creature!"

Harry eyed her with loving tolerance. "That's because you can see nothing but good in anyone, loveliest of creatures!"

For once Perdita found their affectionate small talk irritating. She changed the subject. "Harry, have you come across Bertram at all recently?" He looked so immediately uncomfortable that she didn't wait for him to reply. "Yes, I can see that you have. Has he been running up debts?"

Harry, relieved of the necessity to fabricate some acceptable half-truth, gave a resigned shrug. "Well, to tell the truth, he has become a bit of an embarrassment in the last day or two. He latched on to me from the first—a face he knew and all that—"

"Harry lent him money," Amaryllis blurted out, and received an impatient look from her husband. "Well, I think Perdita ought to know," she insisted. "Not because you begrudge it, but because that was the beginning of it in a way—"

"Tillot said that he was temporarily short of funds," Harry explained. "Said you'd been about to make arrangements for him to draw on your bank when the accident happened."

"Yes, I see," Perdita said. And then, quietly, "How much did he borrow, Harry?"

He looked affronted. "Dammit, a fellow don't go blabbin' about such things!"

"But I must pay you back! I'll warrant he hasn't, nor ever intends to. Oh, it really is too bad of Bertram!"

"Lord, I didn't begrudge him the money! Reckoned he deserved it, doing what he'd done, saving your life and all." Harry grinned sheepishly. "And I wasn't alone in thinking that. I daresay there were any number of houses in Bath last week where he could count on being offered *carte blanche*. Only—"

"Only he took unwarrantable advantage of the hospitality offered? Oh, you needn't look like that, Harry. I know Bertram only too well. Besides, Lord St. Ive said something very similar." She looked him straight in the eye. "What I don't know is how heavily he has plunged."

Harry shrugged and ran nervous fingers through his sandy hair. "Well, you know how it is. I introduced him to Grantly—he likes to rattle the bones a bit." He heard Perdita's stifled groan. "Yes, well, I suppose it wasn't a wise move, on reflection, because Grantly introduced him to one or two of his particular gaming cronies, some of them hard cases, and—"

"Oh no!" Perdita could imagine the rest.

Harry grimaced. "Luckily, Tillot had this ring to pledge—said it had belonged to his mother, and he was loath to part with it. I only know what happened because Grantly told me—I say, love, are you all right? You're looking a bit pale. Isn't she looking pale, Amaryllis?"

"Too many visitors," Amaryllis exclaimed with a rush of sympathy. "And I shouldn't wonder if you've tired her out with your depressing stories!" She looked pointedly at Harry. "Anyhow, we really ought to be *going*."

He looked at her in some surprise. "Ought we?" And then, as realization dawned. "Oh yes, of course. Look, old girl, don't fret about Tillot. It'll all come right in the end, you'll see."

"What?" Perdita came to as from a dream. "Yes,

I'm sure it will. Do you really have to go?" But when they insisted, she didn't press them.

When they had gone, she went slowly upstairs to her bedchamber, and across to the small chest of drawers beside her dressing table. She opened the topmost drawer and took out her jewel case. The space reserved for the emerald ring that had been a coming-of-age gift from her grandfather was empty. She went through the motions of turning out the entire contents for a thorough search, knowing all the time that it would be a waste of time. She sat down on the bed, feeling a trifle sick. Then she carefully replaced everything and slowly left the room. As she reached the head of the stairs she became aware of someone watching her, and turning, saw Bertram's valet, Bridge, standing in the shadows. He was small, bland-faced, and sallow, and perhaps because she was feeling so low, he seemed to exude a faint air of menace.

"Were you wanting something?" she asked, more sharply than she intended.

He bowed his head with a hint of subservience that didn't quite ring true. "No, madam. Nothing at all, madam," he murmured and melted back into the shadows once more.

Chapter 9

"*W*ELL?" SAID THE DUKE. "Out with it, my boy. What are you waiting for?"

Father and son had barely exchanged half a dozen words on the journey home. The pantomime of getting the duke back into the coach had exasperated both men in differing degrees and for different reasons, and the presence thereafter of Septimus Goring had precluded all but the briefest, most irascible of comments.

Now, however, in the comfort of Anderley Court's blue drawing room, each was free to speak his mind. But the marquis was slow to oblige.

"Very well, then. I'll make a guess at it," continued his father. "You are convinced that not only is my body infirm—my wits have finally gone a-begging, too!"

"Not so, sir." The marquis flushed. "I have the greatest respect for your grace's intellect—it would be a foolish man who underestimated it."

"I am relieved to hear you say so," murmured the duke. "Yet you find my friendship"—his eyes glinted sardonically—"with Perdita unseemly, even a trifle ridiculous at my advanced age, perhaps?"

Flicked on the raw by his father's tone, the marquis said through shut teeth, "I think that, confined as you have of necessity been, it is all too easy to be misled."

"By a pretty face, you imply. So be it. You are entitled to your opinion. Nonetheless, you will lend me your support in sorting out this unsavory cousin of Perdita's?" It was phrased with the exquisite politeness of a question, but St. Ive knew that his acquiescence was taken for granted.

Miss Perdita Grant had well and truly ensnared his father, and it was not difficult to see why. True, she was not heart-stoppingly beautiful in the way that Amaryllis was, but she had a delicate natural beauty that was curiously seductive. He only wished that he might be able to find her sufficiently lacking in other qualities to compensate, but, though it irked him to admit it, her appeal was formidable. She had poise, humor, and a kind of bright fearless tenacity in adversity that aroused his reluctant admiration, in spite of his bitter mistrust of her. There had been a brief moment that very afternoon when, seeing her so pale still, and unexpectedly vulnerable in her blacks, he had known an overwhelming urge to loose the pins confining her neatly braided hair; had remembered how the silvery cascade spilled like silk across his sleeve when he had carried her in his arms, and the curious pang of apprehension he had felt to see her so still and white, the spirit all drained out of her.

But these were treacherous thoughts. How could he blame his father for succumbing if he, likewise, should prove less than immune from temptation? He ruthlessly reminded himself of her less agreeable traits—her irrational stubbornness, a tendency to flippancy which, allied to an at times unwomanly forwardness, seemed to characterize her determination to become Duchess of Anderley at

whatever cost. She was clever, too. It would not do
to underestimate her—or the subtlety of her hold
on his father.

But she should not succeed, he vowed, not while
he was around to stop her. And stop her he would.
He too could be subtle, as she would discover to
her cost.

"Well, Piers?"

He was, all at once, remarkably sanguine. "Oh,
I'll play my part, never fear."

SO IT CAME ABOUT that some hours later the Marquis of St. Ive was being admitted to a fine man-
sion on the outskirts of Bath, just off the London
Road. The furnishings were of the very best, but
he had little time to admire them before being
ushered through into a small saloon at the rear of
the hall by his host, Sir James Longton, a gentleman with several chins and an air of false geniality.

"There you are, my lord," he gushed. "We had
almost given you up! I said to Lord Grantly, 'Vyvian,
my lad, either your directions were hopelessly out,
or his lordship has changed his mind!' But you are
here now, and deeply honored I am to welcome so
prestigious a guest! You will not mind if we go
straight in? The others are eager to begin."

St. Ive swallowed a strong urge to say something
cutting, apologized for his lateness—a trifling problem with his curricle—and, lying in his teeth, expressed his pleasure at having been invited to Sir
James's, where he had been assured of play such
as one seldom found outside London.

The introductions were brief, some of the seven
gentlemen there being slightly known to him already. He met Bertram Tillot's eyes without a flicker
of recognition, and the other, already half in his
cups, showed no sign of having seen him before.

Only Grantly greeted him with any degree of familiarity.

The game was deep basset, and the atmosphere was soon tense, almost claustrophobic, for those present were mostly hardened gamesters. St. Ive held his own for the first hour and then began to win steadily. And his eyes beneath lowered lids, apparently intent upon the cards, watched Bertram Tillot grow ever more erratic—a run of luck making him careless so that he lost all he had gained and was soon scrawling IOUs with increasing frequency. As he lost, he drank, so that by the time the game broke up St. Ive was comfortably in pocket, and held a considerable number of Bertram's notes. The young man's face was flushed with wine and excitement as he muttered something about some slight delay in paying his dues, which caused a wry exchange of glances among their companions.

To everyone's surprise the marquis seemed prepared to be magnanimous. He waved aside a pithy comment by one who had cause to know all about Bertram's slight delays. "I'm always willing to accept a gentleman's word until I find it proved false," he said. His eyes were narrowed so that Bertram couldn't be sure whether or not he was smiling as he continued blandly, "I wonder—would you care to come back with me for a drink? You go my way, I believe? The other side of Bath—on the road to Twerton? You won't mind riding in a curricle?"

Amid astonished glances, Bertram preened, his ego puffed up no end at finding himself being courted by this acknowledged nonpareil—it only proved that it took a true nobleman to know how to treat one with style. He had, he explained reluctantly, come in his gig (that it belonged to Perdita had long since slipped his mind), which was a pity, for he would very much like to have ridden in a bang-up rig such as Lord St. Ive would no doubt be running.

"Well, that is no problem, surely?" said the marquis, not by a quiver betraying his distaste of such encroaching manners. "Sir James will have no objection to your leaving it here overnight, I hope, and there is nothing to stop you riding over for it tomorrow."

The puzzled baronet clearly thought him addle-brained, but agreed readily enough, and so it was arranged.

There were many times during the ensuing journey, which passed without a word being exchanged, when Bertram came to regret his decision, and never more so than when, outside the confines of the town, he discovered that not only did his lordship drive to an inch, but did so at a speed which, in the darkness that prevailed, seemed to him to verge on the suicidal and left him feeling devilish queasy. Worse still, his one protest had been met with a short bark of laughter that, to his oversensitive ears, sounded little short of maniacal! He came as close as he had ever done to praying.

It was with an overwhelming sense of relief, therefore, that he at last became aware of a slight slackening of pace. Then they were swinging in between huge gateposts and after the better part of another mile came to a halt before a short flight of steps leading to a shadowed portico. He stumbled up them, feeling as though his legs did not belong to him, and found that beyond them all was filled with light; a handsome hall and handsome staircase which with much concentration he negotiated without mishap, and at last a drawing room—cool, elegant, with any number of blue velvet chairs into which one might sink.

Before he could select one, however, someone coughed. Over by the fireplace someone was sitting—not the marquis, surely? He peered closer. The likeness was quite marked, and yet . . .

St. Ive's voice, coming from directly behind him, seemed to settle the point, but it seemed to have lost its note of cool amiability. "Mr. Tillot—pray allow me to make you known to my father, his grace, the Duke of Anderley."

Anderley. Bertram's by now befuddled mind grappled with the familiar-sounding name, and then cleared with startling suddenness. Of course! Anderley, Perdita's neighbor. Somehow he had never connected the marquis with . . .

He straightened up, moved a nervous hand to check the set of his cravat, and bowed. "Y-your grace."

"Mr. Tillot," said the duke in a voice that chilled him to the bone, "you had better sit down. We have a great deal to talk about—or rather, I will talk, and you will listen."

BERTRAM TILLOT ARRIVED back at Marston Grange in the early hours of the morning, battered in mind and spirit, having experienced the worst, most humiliating experience of his life, and physically exhausted from having had to make his own way back from Anderley Court—the longest distance he had covered on his own two feet since boyhood—in a rainstorm.

His valet, Bridge, heard him arrive and went down to him at once. He scarcely recognized his immaculate master in the bedraggled creature who stood shaking the rain from himself in the middle of the hall floor.

"Oh, sir!" he said, deeply shocked. "Your Hessians, sir. They are covered in mud!"

"Well, of course they damn well are! What do you expect, dolt?" Bertram, in the grip of near-hysteria, turned on the hapless valet, venting upon him the kind of tongue-lashing he himself had received at Anderley's pleasure somewhat earlier, the indignity of which had had ample time to fester within him. He had been duped by that two-faced St. Ive and humiliated by his cold devil of a father, and at the end of it all had been turned out without offer of transport into a wetting mizzle which had grown steadily heavier.

"The walk will help to clear your head," the marquis had said with an appalling indifference that had nurtured seeds of revenge in Bertram's tortured mind as he stumbled away. Of course, it had been a mistake to attempt the shortcut favored by Perdita—acceptable in daylight and on horseback, it proved to be full of hazards, and with the increasing rain, soon became knee-deep in places in wet, foul-smelling undergrowth. By the time he reached home his grudge had reached obsessive proportions and had expanded to embrace his treacherous bitch of a cousin who had doubtless put them up to it.

When Perdita heard the shouting, she was not immediately aware of whether it was a dream or reality. But suddenly she was wide awake. It took but a moment to assure herself that the disturbance was no figment of her imagination, then she was pulling on her dressing gown and hurrying to the stairs. Below she found Fletcher hovering in some distress, his authority somewhat diminished by the incongruity of his night apparel, crowned as it was by a tasseled nightcap.

"I can't tell you how sorry I am that you have been disturbed, Miss Perdita," he said, the slight quiver in his voice betraying his agitation. "Only I can't make Mr. Tillot heed me. I have tried, but he called me—" Here the old butler's mouth trembled, and Perdita hastened to stem his shaming admission.

"Go back to bed, Fletcher," she told him gently. "I will deal with Mr. Tillot."

"Oh, but ma'am—I cannot permit you to be subjected to such violent abuse! He might well strike out—"

"It's all right," she reassured him. "He won't harm me, I promise you."

The sheer force of Bertram's invective had carried the two men into the passage beyond the book room, the valet huddled into an attitude of passive endurance, as of long practice, which made Perdita wonder why he put up with such treatment. It wasn't even as if he got paid regularly.

She waited for a lull in the proceedings, then said calmly and clearly, "Bertram, be quiet."

He stopped in midsentence, and slowly turned. Perdita had not expected such instant obedience and for a moment was almost at a loss, the more so as he did indeed present a ludicrous appearance which at any other time might have tempted her to smile. But the venom in his eyes drove all thought of humor from her mind.

"Well, *sweet coz*, so you are here! Have you come to gloat?"

There was a curious lightness in his voice that was more disturbing than out-and-out anger. She schooled herself to disregard it.

"I have no idea what you are talking about, but I do take great exception to having the house disrupted at this hour with your disgraceful tantrums," she said coldly. "I must insist that you control yourself immediately."

"And if I don't? Have me thrown out, will you?" he sneered. "It must be my night for it! I've been thrown out of better places than this, let me tell you. Anderley Court, for instance. But I don't need to tell you that, do I?"

She sighed. "I don't know what you're talking

about, Bertie, but you are clearly in your cups and
incapable of rational conversation. Go to bed and
we'll talk in the morning."

Her attitude seemed only to inflame him. " 'Go
to bed, Bertie,' " he mimicked savagely. " 'Pay your
debts—get out of town—stand on your head'—God!
What ingratitude!" He peered into her puzzled
eyes. "Playing Miss Innocent, are we? I'm talking
about your tame duke and his unscrupulous son!"

He swung his sodden beaver hat in a wild arc,
and it caught a small Grecian figurine standing in
an alcove, bringing it crashing to the floor. Perdita
uttered a gasp of dismay as the head snapped off
and rolled against the wall. "Ha! How is that for a
symbolic gesture? Maybe I should have let that
stone pediment fall on you, after all—then all my
problems would have been solved!"

"Bertram Tillot, that is an obscene and evil sup-
position! Be silent at once!"

Miss Midgely had come downstairs, unnoticed
by either of them, and stood there in her severely
practical night attire, looking stern and immovable.

Bertram bowed with bitter mockery. "I might
have known you'd not be far away, you old gorgon!
Always there, aren't you? Protecting your charge—
and your own interests, belike! That's all I need,
dammit—petticoat tyranny!"

"You are disgusting!" said Miss Midgely. "Perdita,
come away and leave him. You will get no sense
out of him tonight."

Feeling slightly sick, Perdita stooped to pick up
the broken figure.

"Leave it," Bertram snarled. "You can always
buy another. But what about me? Out on my ear,
thanks to your treacherous scheming. Packed off
on the first stage to London—after I've paid my
creditors, of course, and that precious marquis will

be there to see I don't renege. What a way to show your gratitude, *coz*!"

Perdita flinched, but remembering the ring, hardened her heart. "All right, Bertie, there is obviously much I don't know, so we'd better have the whole thing out now." She opened the door to the book room and went in. There was still a faint glow from the dying fire, and she walked unerringly toward it in the darkness, running her hand along the mantelshelf in search of the taper and finding it, then thrusting it into the embers in order to light the branches of candles on either side of the mirror. Her face stared back at her, a pale blur in the shadowy glass.

"Come in, Bertie," she said calmly.

He did so, suddenly bereft of words, subsiding like a spent balloon. But not so Midge, who followed on his heels, outrage in every line of her.

"This is the most ridiculous thing I have ever known! Perdita, this is madness—not to say quite improper!"

For the first time a gleam of humor flickered in Perdita's eyes. "Dear Midge! How like you to remind me of that. But truly, I think I am in no danger, either physically or morally!" She glanced at Bertram as she spoke, and it certainly seemed that he had exhausted his wrath, for he was already slumped dejectedly in a chair. She lowered her voice. "Do please leave me alone with him—he may not speak half so freely with you here, and there are things that I must know."

Chapter 10

*P*ERDITA SLEPT LATE the next morning, but even
so, she was up and had breakfasted before
Bertram appeared, looking sickly and subdued, and
regarding the table and its contents with a jaun-
diced eye.

In other circumstances Perdita might have felt a
twinge of pity for him, but he had behaved despi-
cably and had brought most of his troubles down
on his own head, so she felt no compunction about
leaving him to brood.

She had already broken it to Midge that she was
going out. "I want to go to Anderley," she said. "And
as soon as possible."

"I suppose I may know better than to ask why,"
the other said with one of her direct looks.

Perdita felt guilty. "My dear, I will explain all
later, I promise. It's just a little complicated!"

"It's that right enough," said Miss Midgely dryly.
And then, "Oh, go along with you. Do you think I
don't know by now that when you are set on a
course of action, no power on earth—certainly no
argument of mine—can move you from it? Just so
long as I am not required to be civil to that young
man, for that I do draw the line at!"

"I don't think Bertram will feel much like talking this morning, Midge dear," Perdita prophesied, and she went to order the carriage, being as yet unfit to ride.

She had taken a great deal of trouble with her appearance, for she was going to need every ounce of confidence that she could muster, and it had long been her experience that she was best able to acquit herself when everything else about her was right. Even so, several times during the relatively short journey she caught herself twisting the strings of her reticule into knots, and was obliged to unravel them.

Pendlebury was surprised to find her arriving at the front door, though he was quick to mask his expression, his portly figure bending a little stiffly in salute as he expressed his pleasure upon seeing her fully recovered.

"Why, thank you," she said, smiling warmly to hide her ridiculous nerves. "Is his grace about yet, do you know?"

Before Pendlebury could answer, St. Ive's voice came floating across the hall. "Miss Grant—you are about early!"

He was descending the stairs in an unhurried way, dressed with that indefinable hint of casual elegance that Bertram would never achieve. He nodded to Pendlebury to leave them and took her arm in a deceptively gentle clasp. "Come into the library and sit down. I hope you may not have tired yourself."

"Thank you, my lord, but I am not a fragile flower!" she retorted. It was hardly an auspicious beginning.

"No," he agreed pleasantly. "More of a holly bush, really, I suppose. Do sit down."

She did so, swallowing her annoyance, and then, meeting his eyes, bit back a reluctant laugh. "I'm sorry, but you can have no idea how tedious it can become, to be forever cosseted! As if one hadn't the sense to know one's own capabilities."

"I can imagine," he murmured, taking the chair opposite her. "So I shan't even trouble to inquire how you are feeling. You were asking for my father, I believe? He isn't about yet, I'm afraid. May I be of any help?"

This was exactly what she had hoped to avoid. She would by far rather have spoken to the duke, daunting as that would have been. But it could not be helped.

"I have come about my cousin," she said.

"Yes, I rather thought that might be it." He crossed one immaculately buckskin-clad leg over the other and draped his arm across the back of his chair in a careless fashion. She waited for him to continue, but he, it seemed, was doing likewise, a look of polite expectancy on his face.

It was a pleasant room, she thought inconsequentially, looking about her as if for inspiration—the paneling in light polished oak, and the books protected by doors of prettily latticed glass. It had none of the gloom she associated with many libraries. Her glance in the course of its travels inevitably clashed at last with those cool blue eyes, intent upon her. The moment could be delayed no longer.

"When I agreed to let the duke deal with Bertram," she began, "I had no idea that matters would move so swiftly, or that he would be so . . . ruthlessly dealt with!"

"You think my father was too ruthless?"

She drew in a quick little breath, her glance still locked with his. "I have begun to wonder just how much is attributable to the duke, and how much to you."

"I see."

Perdita had expected him to take issue, but he

just sat there, almost insolently at ease, watching her.

"Well, how would you like to be treated as you treated Bertram last night? Quite apart from anything else, he was soaked to the skin when he got back!"

"A little rain never hurt anyone," he said imperturbably. One eyebrow lifted in faint surprise. "Do I take it that you were witness to his return, late as it was?"

"Considering all that had happened," she said tartly, "it is hardly to be wondered at that he woke the house."

"And naturally he told you how he had fared?"

"In graphic detail." She was on surer ground here. "How *you* lured him back to Anderley in the most despicable way—how *you* are to escort him into Bath later this morning and are to provide him with money drawn on his grace's bank with which to pay his creditors, of whom *you* have furnished yourself with a complete list." She paused for breath.

"And is that the sum of what he told you?" His voice was quite expressionless.

"Almost. Except that for the addition of a further consideration, he is required to pack his bags and leave here—to return at his peril."

"Forgive me, but isn't that what you wanted?"

Perdita stirred uncomfortably. "Yes, but not like this!"

"In view of the callous way he has taken advantage of you and jeopardized your good name, I would say that Tillot has fared rather better than he deserves." The marquis uncrossed his legs and sat forward suddenly, and it was all she could do not to jump. "Incidentally, do rid yourself of the notion that any of this has my approval, Miss Grant. My father enlisted my help, and I gave it—reluctantly, out of consideration for his disability, not because I endorse his quixotic behavior. For my part, I wouldn't have vouchsafed Tillot one penny piece beyond the price of a ticket on the first available stage out of Bath! If I were you, I would thank heaven fasting for my father's absurd generosity and leave well alone!"

This cutting indictment was too much. Perdita sprang to her feet. "But you are not me, my lord, and I thank God for it! Furthermore, I deeply resent your interference in my affairs!" He too had risen and was standing over her in a manner calculated to intimidate, but she was too incensed to care. "For your information, it is not and never has been my intention to allow his grace or anyone else to pay my cousin's debts. That would be iniquitous!"

"Then what in heaven's name *did* you expect of my father?"

She shrugged helplessly. "I thought he would talk to Bertram—put the fear of God into him, if you like. Make him understand that he must go away."

He didn't believe her. It was patently evident in the way he was staring down that impossible nose at her. She stared back defiantly.

"Well, what's done is done," she said. "My purpose in coming here this morning is to ask you for that list you compiled of Bertram's debts."

"For what purpose?"

She quelled exasperation. "I should have thought that was obvious."

"I fear it is. You can hardly mean to settle them yourself, for that would call down a spate of gossip. So I presume you mean to trust Tillot with the money and hope he will not cheat you yet again?" He shook his head in mock sorrow. "Don't chance it, Miss Grant. Unless he has someone like me at his back, I wouldn't give that"—he snapped his fingers in her face—"for your expectations!"

Perdita flushed, uncomfortably aware that he was right, and resenting him the more for it. "The risk would be mine," she said stubbornly. "But I do acknowledge the sense of what is proposed—"

"You do?"

She ignored the sardonic glint in his eyes. "I am not a fool, my lord, though it might please you to think it. But without the list, I cannot repay his grace, and that I *am* resolved to do."

He stood for a moment looking down at her without speaking, his face, set against the light, planed in strong autocratic lines, a slight furrow between his narrowed eyes. Perdita was a little oppressed by his nearness, by the sheer force of personality contained beneath that casual exterior. Only a determination not to be over-awed enabled her to look back at him steadily.

"Then you must fight it out with my father. I am only his instrument in the affair."

Her reluctant acquiescence should have ended the matter, but he made no attempt to move, and something in the way he was regarding her sent a vague flutter of panic through her. She half turned away only to be pulled back, not roughly but quite inescapably, his long slim fingers sliding down her arms to encircle her wrists.

He had expected her to struggle and was intrigued when she did not. She stood, quiescent, those clear gray eyes holding his fearlessly—well, not quite fearlessly, perhaps, for if one looked closely there was just a hint of something lurking in their cool depths, something that was echoed in the color that came and went in the pure oval of her face, framed by the gray silk ruching that lined her bonnet brim, while under his fingers he could hardly fail to be aware of the blood thudding in her veins.

"Must we be enemies?" he asked softly.

There was a curious restriction in Perdita's throat which made answering difficult. "I . . . have no wish to be at odds with you, my lord. Indeed, I would be happy to bury our differences. And it would please his grace."

"Would it?" he murmured, a strange inflection giving the words an ambiguity she couldn't fathom. '*Are* you in love with him, I wonder?"

She forced a lightness into her voice. "You can hardly expect me to answer that, sir."

An appreciative glimmer of humor came into his eyes. "I suppose not, but there are more ways than one of testing your constancy."

"No!" The sudden wild panic with which she tried to tug her hands free betrayed that she had read his intention only too clearly. "Even you would not stoop that far to play your father false!"

"Which only goes to show how little you know of me." His soft laugh mocked her. "It would be so easy to convince myself that I was acting in my father's best interests!"

Perdita was out of her depth and floundering. Until now it had always been she who had retained the initiative in her relationships with those gentlemen of her acquaintance who fancied themselves attracted to her, able to laugh them out of any tendency to overeffusiveness. But St. Ive was not like anyone she had ever encountered, except perhaps his father, in whom she had occasionally glimpsed this same kind of predatory intensity. She blushed now, remembering how, from a distance, she had watched its effects upon others with amusement.

There was no doubt in her mind that St. Ive was amusing himself now at her expense, just as she knew there was no hope of extricating herself if he did not wish it; certainly he would not be laughed out of it, and she very much doubted she could shame him, though it had to be attempted. Fighting was so undignified.

She abandoned the unequal struggle to free herself. "Very well. If you hope that I will fight and plead, you are quite out. My strength is so obviously inferior to yours that I could not hope to win. Therefore, you must do as you will."

"Must I?" for a moment he was taken aback, his eyes widening to meet her challenging gaze. Then he smiled, wickedly amused. "The woman tempted me, Lord," he murmured, and easily encompassed both her wrists in one hand while with the other he reached up and loosed her bonnet strings, pushing it back until it tumbled to the chair behind her.

It was all accomplished without hurry, yet Perdita scarcely had time to draw breath before his mouth closed on hers. His free hand cupped her head, drawing her ever closer; sensations of outrage welled up and died almost as soon as they had come, making way for other, much stranger sensations. His mouth grew more insistent, and she found herself responding with a shamelessness that she was powerless to prevent.

At last he released her—steadied her as she half stumbled, not knowing where to look. It was his laugh that signaled a return to sanity, a soft triumphant laugh deep in his throat that brought the humiliating color flooding to her cheeks. Without stopping to think, she raised her hand and slapped his face with all the strength she could muster, oblivious of the jar to her shoulder, and he, unprepared for the swiftness of her reactions, had no time to evade the blow.

He did, however, catch the flying hand that delivered it, seizing it in a bruising clasp that held her rigidly unmoving. He was still smiling, but now it was a pitiless travesty of a smile that struck

fear into her. In mounting horror she saw the
mark of her hand turn bright red on his face.
Never in her life had she raised her hand in anger!
Yet the thought of apologizing did not for a moment enter her head.

St. Ive's reactions were less straightforward. Fury
at the affront to his pride was uppermost, a wild
unreasoning fury that refused to admit his own
culpability; and faced with her continuing unshrink-
ing defiance, he would accept nothing less than
her complete subjugation. With a muffled oath he
jerked her forward roughly and heedless of her
skirl of pain, claimed her mouth again, using her
with utter ruthlessness until at last it dawned upon
him that she was as impassive as a rag doll in his
arms. Appalled by his own unbelievable insensitiv-
ity, he let her go, noting with a curious pang how
she winced as she bent to pick up her bonnet with
trembling fingers.

"Oh, damn! Your shoulder . . ." he began in
self-disgust, but she would not allow him to finish.

"It's all right," she said, without looking at him.

"Don't be a little fool!" he exclaimed savagely as
it became apparent after her halfhearted attempt
to put the bonnet on that she could ill manage it.
He took it from her, his face rigidly set as she
stood passively while he drew it over her disar-
ranged hair and tied the ribbons under a chin
that remained resolutely unyielding. "Miss Grant—
Perdita—"

"No!" Her voice was stifled, but firm. "Please,
just let me go!"

He shrugged and stood aside to let her pass,
then moved to open the door for her. A few moments later he stood at the window watching as
her carriage vanished from sight, his fingers absently massaging his cheek, which still stung
slightly, his thoughts in turmoil. Finally he flung

away from the window and sprawled in a nearby chair. "Damn!" he exclaimed with soft vehemence. "Damn, damn, damn!"

IN THE PRIVACY of her carriage, Perdita sat stiffly in a corner with the back of her hand pressed against her mouth, swallowing convulsively over the constricting lump in her throat, and feeling as though every nerve in her body had been set on fire. She closed her eyes and leaned her head against the squabs. For almost the first time in her life she had lost control—of her temper, her emotions, and, far worse, her will. And for that St. Ive was to blame. She would never forgive him!

By the time she reached home the worst of her distress had passed and she was able to achieve a measure of composure sufficient to get her by, though Midge observed with tart ambiguity that some people had little more sense than to go around looking for trouble. This produced a rather choked laugh, but as Fletcher was hovering, waiting to know what was to be done with Mr. Tillot's baggage, which Bridge was wishful to bring down into the hall, Perdita was saved the trouble of answering. And with Bertram still indulging in a fit of the sullens, her own preoccupation was hardly noticed.

She had already raised with him the matter of her emerald ring, which he had at first denied all knowledge of, suggesting that one of the servants must have stolen it.

"That sly little thing that creeps about the place. She ain't been here above a week or two," he said with ill-concealed spite. "Comes from a penniless family, I shouldn't wonder—a great temptation, leaving jewelry around with folk like that in the house. You should keep it locked up, coz."

Any lingering guilt Perdita had felt about him vanished at that point. "Not only do I know that you took it," she said coldly. "I could, with a discreet amount of questioning, discover where and when you pledged it. However, I would much prefer that you spared me the trouble."

He had shrugged, but she was left with the uneasy feeling that though he was not averse to having his gambling debts paid, he might cavil at wasting good money redeeming a ring, especially one that would not be his to pledge again in the future. Perhaps she could ask Harry to make inquiries.

She was dreading the moment when the marquis would arrive to collect Bertram. Would it be outright cowardice, she wondered, if she pleaded a headache and retired to her room? Midge could perfectly well deal with him. She suspected that he had found favor in Midge's eyes, for she spent much time praising his kindness and helpfulness during Perdita's illness.

"Now there is a true gentleman," she declared, a fact which seemed to her to be born out by his offer to take Bertram into Bath. "For I shouldn't suppose he has much in common with that rogue!"

Oh, if only she knew the half of it, Perdita thought.

As matters turned out, however, Bertram's departure was achieved with the minimum of contact between herself and the marquis, she being much occupied in taking leave of her cousin while he conversed briefly with Miss Midgely, so that any lack of conversation between them passed unnoticed. St. Ive was using the duke's traveling coach, in order to accommodate the baggage, and Perdita couldn't help smiling a little to see Bertram's step take on the hint of a swagger as he approached this elegant equipage. Bridge was already sitting stiffly on the box with the coachman, clutching the bag containing his own few valuables tightly to his chest.

St. Ive took his leave of both women as briefly as politeness would allow, and he was on the point of climbing into the coach when Perdita nerved herself to run forward.

"My lord?"

He turned at once, frowning. "Miss Grant?"

She said, almost gabbling the words, "There is a ring, an emerald . . . it is very important to me. Bertram pledged it, I don't know where . . . but I don't trust him to redeem it. Would you . . . could you, if it isn't too much trouble . . ."

She forced herself to look at him, and rather wished she hadn't.

"I'll do what I can," he said tersely, and turning away, swung himself quickly into the coach. A lackey put up the steps and closed the door.

Chapter 11

WITH BERTRAM'S DEPARTURE, life very quickly settled back into its former pattern and the house once more became a peaceful retreat with no untoward events to disturb it. Miss Midgely made no secret of her own satisfaction.

"That young man had a disrupting influence even when he was not here," she told Mrs. Windlesham. "One always had the feeling that sooner or later there would be trouble."

"And yet one cannot but be glad that he *was* here, for poor dear Perdita's sake!" Mrs. Windlesham shuddered. "Still, we must not be brooding upon what might have been. She has certainly made a splendid recovery, though I'm sure that in her place I would not be venturing out on horseback so soon."

Almeria Midgely privately shared this view, but not for anything would she admit as much to her visitor. "I long ago gave up trying to persuade Perdita out of doing something once she had set her heart on it, and in this case I really was not sorry when Dr. Bryant pronounced her fit to ride, for I had grown quite weary of watching her, so full of the fidgets was she!"

"It is most unlike her to be so restless, and cattish, is it not? She was quite short with me not two days since when I ventured to mention that Lord St. Ive had returned to London. Mr. Windlesham is of the opinion that the mere fact of being confined must be irksome to someone like Perdita, and I daresay he is right, because she does like to be beforehand with the news—especially when it concerns his grace. I suppose it is to Anderley that she had gone this afternoon?"

Perdita was at that moment sitting with the duke in the garden room and pouring out to him all her frustration. "Honestly, dear sir, you can have no idea how good it was to be on Satan's back again! And I believe he was quite as pleased as I, for although Tom, our young undergroom, has kept him exercised and Bertram took him out occasionally, I doubt he has had a decent gallop for weeks! I took the liberty of riding right across your parkland before leaving him at the stables, and I'm not sure which of us enjoyed it most!"

She stopped to draw breath and became aware that he was regarding her in a highly quizzical way.

"Oh, I'm so sorry!" she exclaimed. "How selfish of me to go on about myself when you are in much worse case than I!"

"Nonsense. Oh, I'm not saying I wouldn't give a great deal to have a horse under me again." The duke's smile was wry. "But I am doing my very best to cultivate a spirit of resignation. Thanks to Goring I may yet walk with some measure of comfort, and must learn to be content with that. It does not come easy."

The last was said with so much feeling that Perdita hardly knew what to say other than to echo his hopes.

"Howsoever," he continued, "I am happy to have you restored to me. Piers returned to London last week, and though I had not thought to say so, I miss him."

Perdita knew St. Ive's name must come up sooner or later, and had schooled herself accordingly. She had not seen him since the day of Bertram's departure. That same evening his groom had returned with her gig, which Bertram had left at Sir James Longton's house, and he had also brought with him a small package containing her ring, and with it a slip of paper. "Miss Grant," the note ran in flowing script, "I am happy to be able to return to you your property. I trust your shoulder will soon mend. St. Ive." In no way could it be construed as an apology, but then she had not expected one, nor was she in any mood to accept one were it offered, so it had come as something of a relief to learn that he was no longer around to plague her.

"I am much beholden to him for the trouble he went to over Bertram," she said now, prepared in his absence to be magnanimous.

The duke chuckled. "Perdita, I am proud of you. You said that almost with conviction."

Her eyes echoed his smile. "Oh, well, I know that he did what he did for you, sir, so that it is really you to whom I owe my thanks. . . ." She hesitated. "And I hope you won't be angry if I ask you to let me know what I owe you." His profile, auster enough in the ordinary way, was forbidding enough to daunt a less tenacious spirit. But Perdita was not such a one. "Dear sir, you must surely see that I cannot allow you to be out of pocket over something that would not have happened had I not been laid up?"

"Humgudgeon, madam!" he said with stark finality. "I refuse to enter into crude bargaining over what is a mere trifle, so let that be an end of it!"

It was at such moments that he was most like his son. The similarity irked her, and angered by his tone, she rose and walked across to the fountain. The golden fish swam lazily among the lily pads, and she found herself envying their uncomplicated existence. He called her name, but she did not immediately answer the imperious summons. Only when his voice softened did she turn at last.

"My dear," he said in more conciliatory tones, "pray allow me the illusion at least of feeling myself to be of some use. I had thought we understood one another rather better."

"Oh, but you are of use!" she exclaimed, hurrying back to him and impulsively giving him her hands. "I for one would be lost without you!"

He looked at her hands with a strange little smile. "As well Piers can't observe us at this moment. He still isn't sure what to make of our . . . relationship." He was silent a moment before saying in a voice curiously devoid of expression, "Still, that won't do him any harm."

This was dangerous ground, and Perdita sought to extricate herself before it became more so. She said diffidently, "If you truly wish to be of use, there *is* a matter that I had been wondering whether to broach."

He was looking quizzical again, and she hurried on before her courage failed her.

"You know I mentioned that I had ridden right across the estate? Well, I hadn't been that way for some considerable time, and I was a little shocked by the condition of the group of cottages that are the homes of your estate workers. The roofing in particular is in a very poor state of repair and must let in the rain shockingly . . . and there is a very general air of neglect."

His brow lifted. "I fail to see what you expect of me. I employ a steward to deal with such matters."

"Yes, well, I don't wish to speak ill of anyone, but if the length of time that Fred Benthall, your steward here, spends in the Anderley Arms is anything to go by, he isn't dealing with them adequately."

Her knowledge of such matters both surprised and amused him. "Your grasp of local affairs is quite masterly, my dear. I won't presume to question how you come to know of Benthall's drinking habits."

Perdita grinned. "My gardener also frequents the Anderley Arms, and is occasionally quite voluble on the subject—particularly as his sister is married to one of your workers." She grew serious. "To be fair, your late wife didn't take much interest, and since her death matters have grown even more lax, so it is hardly surprising if conditions have deteriorated."

"My dear Perdita, I don't pay agents to work only when they are supervised. If Benthall is falling down on the job, then he'll answer to me!"

She bit her lip. "Well, how would it be if you were to drive around that way one day? I will gladly go with you."

"How about now?" he said. "I could do with a little fresh air."

They went in an open landau, to make the most of the spring sunshine, and the duke's keen eyes noted not only the neglect of the buildings pointed out to him by Perdita, but the general run-down state of the whole estate. As they drove his mouth grew thinner, his silences longer, and though the women raised a smile and a curtsy for Perdita, their manner for the most part verged on the sullen.

"Conditions are not easy for them at present," Perdita hastened to explain by way of mitigation.

"I suppose it is an aftermath of the war that prices have soared. Many of them cannot afford even the barest of necessities." She had no way of knowing whether her argument made any impact upon his grace, for he made no reply.

But she had her answer the following week when Benthall was dismissed and a new man appointed.

"I have seldom been so surprised by anything," confessed Mr. Gilles, calling at Marston Grange one afternoon when both ladies were at home. "One would not have supposed that his grace took so much interest."

"It was high time that something was done," said Miss Midgely unequivocally. "Those poor people have been bady used for far too long!"

"I couldn't agree more," said Perdita.

Mr. Gilles blinked, faced with this united front. "The poor are frequently ill used," he said by way of mitigation. "It is their lot, unfortunately."

"That is no excuse for not making a push to help them," Perdita exclaimed. "Personally I am delighted that his grace has taken action."

"Perhaps so, dear ma'am, but one man's gain is another's loss, as you might say, and Benthall is certainly far from delighted. He is quite bitter, in fact, for he has been forced to quit his house and look for other work in order to support his family." The clergyman was gently reproving. "They too are God's children."

Perdita had an innate dislike of being preached at, so that any guilt about the part she had played in the agent's dismissal was swiftly allayed.

"Well, I am sorry for him, of course," she said briskly. "But he would have shown a better care of his family if he had spent less time in the taproom of the Anderley Arms and more doing the job he was paid for."

Nevertheless, she was sorry for the Benthalls. It

could not be pleasant to be obliged to leave a relatively comfortable home, and without a reference a new job would not be easy to find. She rather wished that the duke had been less ruthless— a warning might have sufficed. It was so easy when one saw mostly the more agreeable side of his nature to forget that he could be every bit as unyielding as his son.

When she was dressing for dinner that same evening there was a timid knock at the door of her bedchamber, and to her surprise it was Molly who entered at her bidding.

"Please, ma'am," the young girl said diffidently. "Mr. Fletcher said as I was to come and see you."

The breathless voice tailed off, and Perdita waited expectantly.

"Yes, Molly?" she prompted at last. "Why did Mr. Fletcher send you to me?"

"Well, ma'am, I've just been home . . . it was my day off, you see, and there was something as my dad said . . . and Mr. Fletcher thought you should know . . ."

Again the voice faltered, and Molly's face flushed scarlet. And again Perdita reassured her. Finally it all came out in a rush.

"He . . . my dad, that is, was in the taproom of the Arms last night, and he said that Mr. Benthall was there very drunk, ma'am, swearing something awful, and . . . and . . ." Molly paused, looked apprehensive, and drew a great breath before rushing to a conclusion. "And Dad said as he was damning you, ma'am, as the one who'd put his grace up to it, and saying as . . . how you'd be sorry!"

"Oh dear!" Perdita saw that the girl was acutely embarrassed, and she was careful to keep her voice bright and practical. "Well, thank you for telling me, Molly. Mr. Fletcher was quite right to insist that you should, and I am very grateful to you. But I'm sure we can all forget it now." She smiled. "If one paid heed to everything men say when they have taken too much to drink, life would become very tiresome."

The thought that she had been threatened, however unlikely it was to come to anything, did disturb Perdita vaguely, but she was loath to tell anyone else about it. She caught Fletcher looking at her in a rather troubled way once or twice, and was touched by his concern, but she quietly reassured him, and when it was presently learned that Benthall had secured a position as understeward for a large estate on the other side of Bath, she was pretty sure the whole affair would blow over. There was, however, one uncomfortable moment for her when she drove into Bath a few days later. The carriage was threading its way through a particularly heavy press of traffic near the abbey when she saw Anderley's ex-steward standing at the roadside. Just for an instant her eyes met his, and she was taken aback by the naked malevolence she glimpsed there. And because she was used to being almost universally well liked, it made her sad.

As SPRING CREPT almost imperceptibly into summer, Perdita finally rebelled against her blacks and took to wearing lavender and gray, and although there was no question of her attending the assembly balls, she and Miss Midgely did go to an occasional concert. These diversions, though pleasant, did little to assuage the restless energy that filled Perdita, whose injury was now a thing of the past.

In fact it was now, with the initial harrowing period of mourning at an end, and all her difficulties and upsets associated with Bertram resolved, that she missed her grandfather most keenly. Life seemed depressingly flat and devoid of any expec-

tation of being otherwise. She was filled with yearn-
ings to which she could put no name, and took
refuge in long early-morning gallops on Satan, with
only her groom for company.

It was perhaps mere coincidence that this res-
tiveness came upon her at almost the same time as
she received a letter from Amaryllis, who had gone
to London with Harry for a short visit. It was quite
tiresomely filled with anecdotes about dinners and
balls, and all the people they had met. "Harry met
your cousin at one of his boring clubs, and said he
was as merry as a grig and obviously on a run of
luck. . . . Oh, and who do you think was at Almack's
on Wednesday last? Lord St. Ive! He was being
made much of by Lady Jersey and co., for it is very
seldom that he condescends to honor them with
his company, and makes little secret of the fact
that the tedious rules attached to one's admittance,
to say nothing of the insipidity of the refreshments
and much of the company to be found there, give
him a positive dislike of the place! Only someone
as sought-after as St. Ive could say such things
and not be blackballed! He is being pursued by
Verena Grantly, which amuses Harry no end,
though I cannot but feel guilty, as I am certain he
singled her out in Bath only to divert attention
from me."

Serve him right! Perdita mused with considerable satisfaction. It might teach him not to meddle
in other people's lives. But the letter did unsettle
her for all that. Perhaps it was the thought of all
those dinner parties, the stimulating conversation,
she told herself. She had sometimes wished of late
that Grandpa's aversion to London had been less
rigid, for she had begun to think that she might
rather like its life and bustle—a feeling of being at
the center of things. But her life had been full

enough for all that, and it was this that she now missed.

In an effort to compensate, she threw herself into local affairs with renewed enthusiasm. She had always taken a great interest in the village school, being of the opinion, fostered in her by her grandfather, that only by education would ignorance and want be eradicated. It was not a view shared by everyone, and her frankness had been the cause of many an argument, but since she possessed the happy facility of being able to argue a cause without losing her temper or her ability to see all sides of a question, she had been able to achieve a certain amount of good without incurring ill-feeling.

It was this same espousal of causes that had prompted her to point out to the duke the shortcomings of his steward and the misery that had resulted from it. And it was her enthusiasm that had made him curious to follow the progress of the work that was being done.

He found it a novel and oddly satisfying experience, showing him a side of life that had never until now impinged upon his own. Not that he was a bad landlord. His family seat in Warwickshire was often held up as an example to others of how an estate should be run, but he was well aware that the only credit that could accrue to him was that there he did have an old and trusted estate manager.

But now Perdita's interest and vitality gave him new life. Her visits frequently tempted him out of the house and gave him back something he had thought was gone forever—his spirit, for she mocked him gently, encouraging him to limp with a swagger that she vowed would have all his inamoratas fighting one another for his favors. He did not believe her, but it pleased his ego no end.

And then, one day in July, St. Ive came back to Anderley, bringing with him a small party of friends. Perdita came back with the duke from an inspection of the newly roofed cottages to find Pendlebury in an unaccustomed state of perturbation.

"The devil he has!" said the duke when told. "How many does the small party constitute, Pendlebury?"

"There are six persons in all, your grace," explained the troubled butler. "Including his lordship, that is. I was in something of a dilemma, not knowing how you would wish me to proceed, but in the end I thought it best to ask Mrs. Tonks to prepare the necessary rooms. I hope I did right, your grace?"

"What? Yes, of course. Only thing to do, Pendlebury." The duke nodded. "With any luck they won't stay long."

Perdita, who had experienced a small *frisson* of—what? annoyance-apprehension-panic?—upon hearing the news, said quickly that she would not come up, that it was well past the time that she had told Miss Midgely to expect her, and that no, Pendlebury mustn't think of sending anyone to the stables for her horse—she would enjoy the walk.

Anderley watched this display of very uncharacteristic behavior with amazement, and not a little interest. "It's not like you to run out on company, my dear. As a rule, I'd say there is nothing you enjoy more."

"Yes, but not just at this moment," she said, flustered. "I-I'm not dressed for it, and besides . . ." Her capacity for telling bouncers at the drop of a hat was not great at the best of times. Now her mind was a complete blank.

And the duke was not prepared to give her up without a fight. His eyes were every bit as keen and all-seeing as his son's. "You look charming, as I told you earlier, so that will not suffice as an excuse, and Miss Midgely I am sure does not set her watch by your comings and goings, so unless you can convince me otherwise . . ."

"Don't coerce Miss Grant, Father," drawled the marquis from the stairs. "Her reasons could well be private. Is that not so, ma'am?"

Perdita was mortified to find herself blushing as she murmured assent. His eyes were on her, she knew, though thankfully the duke had turned his attention to his son.

"Dammit, Piers, do you mean to make a habit of turning up unannounced? And bringing half London with you this time! Haven't you got places enough of your own to take them?"

St. Ive looked unrepentant. "I thought you might be glad of a little company."

"Well, I'm not. And next time, be so good as to ask, m'boy."

"Wait until you see," said the marquis cryptically. "You're looking much improved. Miss Grant's ministrations, no doubt?" He turned to Perdita, who was only awaiting the right moment to take her leave. "I'll walk to the stables with you, Miss Grant."

It was the last thing she wanted. "Thank you, but no. You will be wanting to get back to your guests," she said with admirable calm.

"They'll wait," he said as equably as she.

St. Ive's fingers seemed to burn her arm as they walked in silence across the lawns and into the herb garden.

She might have been gratified to know that her effect upon him was almost as dramatic. He had convinced himself that it was his duty to adhere to his original plan to save his father from the wiles of Miss Grant. He had given her every opportunity to deny her interest, but she had if anything chosen to flaunt it before him. A head-on confrontation would clearly get him nowhere; indeed, it seemed to bring out the very worst in both of them. And his earlier attempts to be subtle seemed to have gone woefully awry. So he must try again.

How quiet she was. He glanced down, but the brim of her riding hat shielded most of her face from view. It was, unlike her black one, a wider-brimmed affair in bronze green, sweeping down to one side and adorned with a bewitching feather. Her habit was likewise bronze green; its short close-fitting jacket, curving into her waist, showed her figure to distinct advantage.

"My father was right," he said abruptly. "You do look most charming."

Perdita gave him a startled look and away again. "Thank you." And then, because she had to know, "Why did you bring your friends here?"

He was a long time answering. "Would you believe because I thought it would be good for my father?"

"No," she said, and then, striving to be fair, "At least, that might have been a contributing factor, but it wasn't your main purpose."

His mouth moved in arid amusement. "I see one must add omniscience to your many talents." He felt her arm move impatiently under his hand. "I'm sorry. For once I am not seeking to anger you. In fact, I came with quite the opposite intention—to put the past behind us and begin again, if that is possible."

Perdita slowed to a halt and turned to look up at him. How could one read such a face? It was all planes and angles, his eyes hidden beneath those heavy eyelids. Like father, like son! But at least she had learned how to deal with the duke. With St. Ive, the warning signs were liable to spring up at a moment's notice—danger, keep your distance. And yet she had seen him with Amaryllis, as gentle as a lamb, and even with herself, just for those few moments when she was at her weakest and most vulnerable, he had been kind.

"You ask a lot," she said slowly. "But if you truly mean it . . ."

"I mean it," he said. "The more so since I have seen my father. His improvement is not solely due to Goring's ministrations. He has shed that pall of resignation that surrounded him when first I came, and that I suspect is your doing." His sardonic look was back. "So if I am eventually to call you 'Mother,' there seems little sense in our being enemies." His eyes held hers. "What say you, Miss Grant?"

Chapter 12

'*M*OTHER!"
Perdita almost squeaked the word.

"You hadn't thought of that." His eyes glinted. "The idea doesn't appeal to you?"

The fragrance of thyme was heavy on the air. *I know a bank whereon the wild thyme grows*—the line came unbidden to her mind. The setting was romantical enough, and the gentleman standing before her possessed all the attributes that most young ladies would demand of an Oberon. The incongruity of it all was suddenly too much for her, and she began to laugh.

It was a bubbling infectious sound, the very last reaction St. Ive had expected from her, and though he was a trifle piqued he found his own mouth twitching in response.

"I confess," she gasped when she could draw breath, "that the prospect of having you for a son does give one pause! I shall need to give it very serious consideration if the situation should arise."

"And do you think it will?" he persisted with deceptive sanguinity.

Perdita almost blurted out, "Of course not!" But a perverse desire to keep him in a state of uncer-

tainty made her say instead, with a modest flutter
of her eyelashes, "My dear Lord St. Ive, how am I
to answer that without seeming presumptuous?
You will need to apply to your father if you would
know his intentions."

She could feel his eyes boring into her, but he
said no more, only grasped her arm the more firmly
as they resumed their walk to the stables. Once
there, Satan was led forward by the groom, whose
usual chattiness was quelled by the presence of
his lordship. St. Ive himself threw her up into the
saddle, his expression at its most inscrutable.

"You had better mind how you go, Miss Grant,"
he said with a certain ambiguity. "Fate has a way
of laying traps for the overconfident!"

"Thank you for reminding me, sir," she answered
with a polite inclination of the head. "I shall strive
to remember."

Strangely enough she felt exhilarated rather than
angered by the exchange, and her mood was very
much at one with the intimate hush of the woodland as she left the main drive and allowed Satan
to pick his way unhurriedly through the undergrowth. Deep in thought, she was unprepared for
the sudden jolt when, without warning, Satan
stopped short with a whinny of pain. Only presence of mind and good horsemanship kept her
from going over his head.

"What is it, boy?" she said soothingly, sliding to
the ground as he backed restively, pawing the air
with his right foreleg. She bent down and saw at
once that it was bleeding from a deep cut about
halfway between the knee and the fetlock joint.
The left leg too was grazed, but not so severely.
Hastily she unwound her neckerchief and bound
up the wound before searching for what had caused
it.

She did not have far to look. Hidden by the grasses, a piece of wire was stretched tautly between two trees. Some newfangled vermin trap, perhaps? If so, it was damnably dangerous. Her first instinct was to blame the erstwhile steward—a spiteful retaliation, perhaps, knowing that she rode this way. Except that she had already passed the spot earlier, and either she had been exceedingly fortunate, or the wire had been placed there since. So it looked like the work of one of the junior gamekeepers, or even a poacher, hoping to catch something for the pot.

Perdita toyed with the idea of going back there and then to report it, but she was already more than halfway home, and Satan's leg needed attention as soon as possible. It was unlikely that anyone else would pass this way, so tomorrow would be soon enough.

Mr. Gilles was sitting in the garden with Miss Midgely when Perdita walked through from the stables. He watched her approach, torn between admiration of the splendid picture she presented, so full of vitality and grace, and nervous indecision with regard to the purpose of his visit. Finally he leaned toward Miss Midgely.

"Forgive me, ma'am," he murmured, "I wonder, would you grant me the favor of a word with Miss Grant in private?" He attempted a smile, but his upper lip stuck to his teeth, and the little beads of perspiration glistening along its edge gave him the appearance of an agitated beaver. "I think my purpose will not come as any surprise to you, though my timing might appear to some to be a trifle precipitate. However, in the circumstances . . ."

As Perdita was almost upon them, there was little Miss Midgely could say to dissuade him. She would have liked to tell him that his timing was indeed deplorable, and that if, as she suspected, he meant to preface his proposal with one of his homilies, he might give up all hope of being considered, let alone accepted. Mr. Gilles had been a sad disappointment to Miss Midgely. He had seemed upon first acquaintance to display sufficient good qualities to make him at least a possibility as a husband for Perdita, even though Sir Edwin had been known upon occasion to call him a humbug.

But now even she must perforce admit that he would not do, and could only hope that Perdita would let him down gently. Watching her as she drew near, stripping off her gloves in obvious preoccupation, Miss Midgely felt that the portents were not good.

"Perdita," she called, when it seemed that she would walk right past the bowing clergyman without noticing him. "Here is Mr. Gilles come especially to see you."

Perdita looked up at that, smiling in a vague way that her governess recognized from schoolroom days as signifying that her thoughts were quite elsewhere.

"Is anything wrong, dear?"

She blinked and shook her head as though clearing it. "I'm sorry, Midge. Did you say something? Oh, Mr. Gilles, are you here?"

It was not an auspicious start, decided Miss Midgely.

"Satan has a bad cut," Perdita continued, belatedly answering her question.

"Oh dear! Not too serious, I hope?" inquired Mr. Gilles.

"Bad enough. Sliced almost to the bone. Our groom, George, is doing all he can with it." Perdita frowned, and explained briefly what had happened. "Appalling carelessness on someone's part. I shall have to tell his grace as soon as possible before someone else is hurt."

"Yes, of course."

Out of the corner of her eye, Miss Midgely saw Mr. Gilles making signals to her, and she rose a trifle reluctantly, murmuring about a book she wished to lend their visitor.

Perdita took the seat she had vacated, and Mr. Gilles too sat down. She apologized for her preoccupation and prepared to be entertaining. But he was before her, saying in his "this grieves me more than it does you" voice, "I wonder, dear Miss Grant, have you considered that if you were a trifle less free and easy in your visits to the Court, this sad accident might have been avoided?"

Perdita opened her eyes rather wide at him. "No, I can't say that I have."

"You see, I do feel that you might not have realized how open to misinterpretation your familiarity with his grace appears to . . . other people."

"To you, do you mean?" Perdita said, striving to be civil.

"To others as well. It is one of the considerations that has prompted me to declare myself formally rather sooner than circumstances would normally dictate. I realize that you have been used to going on very much as an independent lady, and indeed when your grandfather was alive, his mere presence sufficed to lend credit to your various enterprises. But Miss Midgely, though a splendid woman, can scarcely be regarded in the same light. . . ."

Perdita, by now only half attending, recognizing in his peroration much that he had said before, had fallen to wondering whether she ought not perhaps to take the gig and go immediately to Anderley Court—if anyone else *should* be hurt, she would hold herself very much responsible.

She brought her attention back to Mr. Gilles in time to hear him conclude piously, 'Our betrothal would of necessity be a quiet affair, and one would not think of putting the banns up until you are out of mourning—"

"I beg your pardon?" she exclaimed, suddenly fully alert.

"I entirely recognize that it would not be seemly to do otherwise," he reassured her hastily. "But the very fact of our betrothal must give a sense of stability to your life—" He got no further.

"Our betrothal? Mr. Gilles, do I take it that you are offering for me?"

"W-why, yes." He seemed puzzled that there should be any doubt. "Surely you knew—we both knew that it was but a matter of time?"

"No." She spoke more abruptly than she had intended, from shock as much as anything. Had she given him any such impression? Surely not. The look on his face made her choose her words less harshly. "I'm sorry, Mr. Gilles. If you have read more into our acquaintance than was there, the fault must have been mine. But there can be no question of a bethrothal between us."

"But—how can this be, dear ma'am? Naturally, modesty has always forbidden you actually to declare your wish to share in my advancement, but it was implicit in the way you have always encouraged me in the belief that I was destined for higher things! We have spoken of it often—"

"No, sir. *You* have spoken of it! If I encouraged your aspirations, it was out of politeness, nothing more, I assure you." Perdita was gentle, but firm, though she was by now wishing him at the devil.

But Mr. Gilles proved tenacious to the end. A note of peevishness had entered his voice. "I do not understand you, ma'am. You cannot prefer to go on as you are . . . with all the restrictions that spinsterhood must impose?"

Really, his pomposity was beyond belief. "I hope

I am not yet at my last prayers, sir," she said with the levity which always made him uncomfortable. "But console yourself that I do at least think more kindly of your proposal, knowing that it arose out of charity, out of pity for my sad state. I had been attributing it to worldly ambitions!"

From the back-parlor window Miss Midgely watched Mr. Gilles leave—stiff-backed and with a face that would turn the cream sour. She went out to Perdita, who still sat, lost in thought.

"He has gone, then?"

Perdita looked up, her mouth twisted in a rueful grimace. "Oh, Midge, I was not as kind to him as I might have been, but he was so complacent!" A hint of a smile came into her eyes. "I rather think I accused him of lusting after my fortune—such as it is!"

Miss Midgely's thin nose twitched, but she said only, "I shouldn't distress yourself overmuch. By now he will have convinced himself that you are not worthy of him."

As a result of Mr. Gilles's visit, Perdita did not go back to Anderley Court that afternoon, promising herself instead that she would drive over the following morning. A further visit to the stables left her in a state of unease, and by morning it was clear to all that Satan's leg was paining him considerably.

"It's early days, Miss Perdita," George said in his unruffled way. "He's a strong healthy 'un, never you fret. He'll get over it."

"Yes, of course he will," she said, but the worry lay at the back of her mind, making her restless. After breakfast she took a basket into the garden to cut some flowers before the sun became too hot, a task guaranteed to soothe. This morning was no exception as the peace, the fragrance, the dew still on the grass dappling her feet, and the contented hum of the bees among the honeysuckle, soon relieved her agitated spirits. With her basket full, she lingered on until, hearing the crunch of wheels, she hurried around to the front of the house in time to see Lord St. Ive's curricle and four being driven to an inch around the curve of the drive by a highly fashionable young gentleman in a voluminous driving coat. At his side the marquis sat, apparently unmoved by the somewhat flamboyant display of driving skill, and as the equipage was brought to a halt at the steps, and a small tiger leaped down and ran to the horses' heads, Perdita was in time to hear the stranger say languidly, "Very creditable, dear old fellow, but your offside wheeler's a trifle sluggish, I'd say."

"It depends who is driving, fribble," returned his host, unimpressed. He swung down lightly and came across to Perdita, very much aware of how well her simple dove-gray dress with its scattering of little white daisies became her fairness.

It was obvious that Freddie Ponsford thought so too. He bowed and returned her welcoming smile with an engaging grin, professing himself delighted to make her acquaintance, and saying how charming she looked with her basket of flowers on her arm.

She led the way into the house and handed the flowers to Molly before taking her guests up to the drawing room, where Miss Midgely sat going through the weekly accounts. She laid them aside, looking for once almost flustered. But Mr. Ponsford had such easy engaging manners that she was very soon at ease again.

The gentlemen declined refreshment, and after the usual politenesses had been exchanged, St. Ive came to the purpose of the visit. "My father has decided to give a dinner party tomorrow evening, and I am charged with the pleasant duty of inviting you both to attend." As Miss Midgely opened her mouth to protest, he stayed her. "His grace charged me most particularly to secure your acceptance, ma'am," he said with a rare smile. " 'Mark my words,' he told me, 'Miss Midgely will try to wriggle out of coming, but on no account are you to allow it.' So you see how I am placed, ma'am?"

Miss Midgely looked uncertainly at Perdita.

"It will be quite informal," St. Ive added by way of persuasion. "Just my own guests and the Windleshams. If you need further persuasion, he said to tell you that with so many young people, he is sorely in need of moral support!"

"Well then . . ." Miss Midgely had turned quite pink.

Perdita, for once very much in charity with his lordship, gave him an approving smile. "Thank your father most warmly, my lord, and tell him that we shall be pleased to attend."

"I expect you will be able to tell him yourself, Miss Grant," he said smoothly. "You won't, I hope, feel in the least awkward about visiting him while my guests are there?"

"Not in the least," she returned with spirit. "As a matter of fact, I had intended to come along later this morning." She explained what had happened the previous afternoon.

"I'm sorry," St. Ive said. "Satan's a fine animal. I wonder—would you allow me to take a look at him?"

"Yes, of course." Perdita was surprised by his concern. "If you like, we can walk around to the stables before you leave."

"No one sounder than Ivo when it comes to dealing with prime cattle," offered Mr. Ponsford. "Ain't much he don't know about treating their various afflictions, either."

In the stables, George eyed the swell gents with misgivings. "I ain't sure as Satan'd take kindly to having strangers in his stall, Miss Perdita." He pulled at his hat. "Beggin' your pardon, m'lord, but he's got a mean way with 'im at the best of times, and what with bein' off 'is oats an' all . . . he might well lash out . . ."

"Thank you for warning me," said St. Ive, undeterred. "Now, if you will be so kind as to unwrap the leg for me?"

George cast a darkling glance at Perdita, who assured him that his lordship knew what he was about. His sniff said clearly that he didn't believe a word of it, but he did as he was bade and stood aside, well out of the way of trouble. But, as he told his cronies that evening in the Arms, "You could've knocked me down! There was 'is lordship on 'is knees without a thought for his fancy breeches, talking to that animal like it was a baby, an' it as meek as you please!"

St. Ive's face gave little away, but Perdita could tell that he was not happy about the state of the wound. "We must act quickly if it's not to turn septic," was all he said. "There's a paste my man Josh uses. I'll send him around the moment I get back." He stood up and absently brushed the straw from his clothes. "You've done a good job," he told George. Then he fondled Satan's ear. "We'll soon have you right, old son." The horse shook its head and whinnied faintly.

"Thank you," Perdita said simply as the two men prepared to drive away. "Satan means a great deal to me."

St. Ive seemed to be frowning slightly, which was hardly reassuring.

"CAN THE ANIMAL be saved?" Freddie asked casually, without taking his eyes from the road. "Leg looked pretty ghastly from where I was standing."

"I don't know. It's odds against, but Josh has worked miracles before."

Freddie flicked out his whip to point the leaders. "You know, she ain't in the least what I expected. Miss Grant, I mean. Devilish attractive young woman . . . not in the least encroaching or brass-faced!"

He got no reply, and looking aside, he saw that St. Ive was still lost in thought. He wondered whether to pursue the subject, but his friend's profile was not encouraging. Instead he gave himself up to the pleasure of tooling as bang-up a rig as he had come across in many a long day. Trust Ivo to have got wind that Dartford was selling his chestnuts before anyone else even knew he was gutted! Picked them up for a song, as like as not!

He negotiated the turn into the grounds of Anderley Court with exemplary skill and had gone for the best part of a mile before St. Ive said suddenly, "Stop just up ahead, will you, Freddie—just here where the drive bends."

"What now?" Freddie asked as his friend jumped down.

"Nothing, dear boy. You can drive on to the stables. I have a fancy to take a stroll in the woods."

Freddie's mouth dropped open. "Stroll in the . . . but dammit, Ivo, you don't even like walking! Well, not just for the sake of it, that is. So, why now?"

St. Ive turned to look up at him, his expression bland. "A whim, dear boy. Just a whim."

"Sounds deuced smoky to me, but I ain't about to argue."

It took the marquis but a few minutes to reach the well-worn path through the trees and trace it back toward the boundary. When he got to within a few yards of the edge, he began to walk with more care, but there was no sign of the wire. Only after retracing his steps several times did he notice the scar freshly scored on the trunk of a tree—and some feet away a second tree, similarly disfigured.

So someone had already removed the wire. One of the keepers, perhaps? Or if not, who?

Chapter 13

*P*ERDITA FOUND HERSELF taking a quite inordinate amount of trouble over her preparations for the duke's dinner party. If only St. Ive's friends proved to be halfway interesting, she was sure she would enjoy it no end.

She had not, after all, driven over to Anderley, her concern for Satan holding her close to home. But she had a visitor in the person of Mrs. Windlesham, who was almost as made up as she by the prospect of dining at Anderley, though for different reasons.

"So generous of his grace to invite Mr. Windlesham and me! I believe that no one else has been asked, other than your good selves," she said happily. "Not that I have not done my very best to visit him throughout the period of his sad affliction, but then one does not perform these little acts of kindness with any expectation of a reward!"

Perdita dared not look at Miss Midgely.

"She really does mean well," she said when Mrs. Windlesham had gone. "For a kinder person one could not wish to meet. If only her tongue did not run away with her so!"

But by evening neither lady had any thoughts to

spare for Mrs. Windlesham. As they approached
Anderley Court each found her heart beating a
little faster—Miss Midgely because she still had
strong reservations about what she insisted upon
calling "stepping out of her class," and though
Perdita reassured her constantly that she could
hold her own in any company, she still could not
think it right or proper. But the only evidence of
nerves was in the way her fingers occasionally
smoothed the skirt of her best black bombazine in
the darkness of the coach.

Perdita, on the other hand, could find no rational
explanation for her own absurd reactions. It was a
dinner party—not even a particularly grand one—
and she had been to hundreds in her time—so
why her heart should be fluttering as though she
were a young girl attending her first ball, she
couldn't imagine.

The duke received them in the blue drawing
room, standing and looking so very *point-de-vice*
with only a slim gold-topped cane for support that
she forgot all else in admiration of him. He took
and held her hand, his twinkling eyes deeply appreciative of her lavender-gray crepe gown with its
brief bodice adorned with silver lace, and the frivolous little cap of silver lace perched provocatively
on her coiled hair.

"Dear sir!" she exclaimed. "It is good to see you
so restored and looking exactly as you did when
we first met!"

"And how *was* he looking then?"

St. Ive's voice at its most sardonic startled her,
but she recovered swiftly, turning a little toward
him, but addressing her words teasingly towards
the duke. "Oh, supremely elegant, charming, and
just a trifle dangerous to know," she said.

The duke chuckled, glanced mockingly at his
son, and kissed Perdita's fingers before releasing

them. "Which only goes to prove what excellent taste you have, my dear."

She looked from one to the other, thinking what a handsome pair they made—both in severe black and white, the duke choosing the formality of knee-smalls while his son wore the slim black trousers favored by the younger fashionables.

"Take Perdita away, Piers, and introduce her to your friends. I shall remain here and talk to Miss Midgely. Pray, be seated, ma'am."

Miss Midgely had been watching him throughout the interchange and had become very much aware of the growing whiteness of his knuckles as he leaned more and more heavily on his cane.

"I will gladly sit, your grace," she said quietly, "if you will do likewise."

For a moment he looked so severe that she thought he would rebuke her for impertinence, but her steady eyes never wavered, and at last, with an abrupt laugh, he capitulated and lowered himself thankfully into the chair immediately behind him. "Why not, indeed? I have made my small gesture of defiance to the gods—no sense laboring the point!"

"No sense at all, your grace," she agreed.

He looked at her in silence for a moment and then smiled faintly. "Would you be offended, ma'am, if I told you that you remind me forcibly of a nanny I once had? She too had the knack of making one feel about so big"—his slim fingers made the appropriate gesture—"if one exhibited the slightest tendency to plume oneself!"

Miss Midgely's eyes twinkled. "I have always thought that gentlemen remain small boys at heart," she said, and had the pleasure of hearing him laugh aloud.

"YOUR COMPANION SEEMS to be getting on famously

with my father," said St. Ive, his fingers firm beneath her arm as they crossed the room. "But I
daresay you don't fear her as a rival."

"Oh, no. Midge would never serve me a back-
handed turn," she said lightly, and had the pleasure of feeling his fingers tighten convulsively.
She was saved from further argument by Mr.
Ponsford, who came forward eagerly to greet her,
and stayed close by her as she later mingled with
the other guests, two of whom—Sir James and
Lady Brant—were slightly known to her through a
mutual acquaintance with whom she and her grandfather had spent several weekends. Sir James was
a genial man in his early forties, and his wife,
pleasant if a little shy. Making up the party were a
Viscount Lyndon and his pretty sister, and Lady
Arabella Winton. And the Windleshams, of course.

It was almost impossible not to stare at Lady
Arabella, who was quite the loveliest creature that
Perdita had ever seen—a mass of luxuriant chest-
nut curls framing a heart-shaped face whose every
feature was perfection, a shapely figure shown to
exquisite effect by a gown of clinging ivory satin.

"Ivo's latest," murmured Mr. Ponsford irrever-
ently. "Rich as bally Croesus and a cit for a husband that don't care who she's with! Damn me if I
know how Ivo manages it—only wish I had half
his address!"

Perdita told herself that she was not shocked by
this revelation of immorality in high places. She
was no green girl and knew well enough that such
things were as commonplace among the *haut ton*
as elsewhere. More so, in all probability. She certainly did not mean to let it spoil her evening.

The dinner passed off very agreeably, and the
gentlemen did not linger long over their port before joining the ladies in the drawing room, but

long enough for Perdita to revise somewhat her opinion of Lady Arabella.

Deprived of the gentlemen's company, she made little effort to converse, and when Mrs. Windlesham was so unwise as to ask her amiably whether she had ever visited Bath before, she opened her violet eyes very wide, drawled, "Lud, I should hope not!" and drifted across to the pianoforte. She was still there when the gentlemen arrived, playing softly to herself, accomplished in that as in all else, Perdita observed uncharitably.

"Come along, Bella—give us a song," urged the viscount, and it was as though someone had turned a switch bringing her back to life. She laughingly obliged, but was much too well bred to perform more than three songs, which she did with wit and charm, before excusing herself. However, it was more than sufficient to make others reluctant to follow her.

"Perdita, my dear, *you* sing most prettily," piped up Mrs. Windlesham in her most carrying voice. A silence fell, and everyone looked her way. "I am sure you will not seek to put yourself forward, but we who have been privileged to hear you will vouch for it! Is it not the case, Mr. Windlesham, Miss Midgely?"

Perdita could cheerfully have strangled the older woman. Her husband murmured agreement, but with a sympathetic glance her way wondered if Miss Grant might perhaps not wish . . . ? Midge gave her the kind of look which as a child she had learned to recognize, and which she now correctly interpreted as "For goodness sake, girl, do as you are bid and stop making such a fuss!" It evoked the same mutinous response that it always had.

More than anyone she was aware of Lord St. Ive still standing near the pianoforte with Lady Arabella at his side, the latter smiling condescendingly at her as Mr. Ponsford took on the mantle of persuader.

"Come, ma'am, you cannot disappoint us!" There was a general chorus of agreement, and glancing around helplessly, Perdita found St. Ive's eyes on her. As her indignation rose, Mr. Ponsford continued eagerly, "Suppose his grace were to command you? You could, sir, could you not?"

The duke had been watching the proceedings in some amusement. "Ah, but would she obey me, my boy? There's the rub. Miss Grant, I fear, has a decided will of her own."

"Oh, good heavens!" Perdita exclaimed, half laughing with exasperation as she capitulated. "What a piece of work over nothing! I only hope you may not be disappointed!"

She left her place beside Miss Lyndon and walked quickly across to the pianoforte, noticing as she did so that Lady Arabella had sunk gracefully into a nearby chair—whence no doubt she hoped to amuse herself at the expense of the provincial nonentity. As for St. Ive, he remained where he was, clearly intending to turn the music for her as he had done for his inamorata.

"Thank you," she said lightly, "I have no need of music."

He lifted a sardonic eyebrow, but made no attempt to move away, leaning instead against the wall in full view of her, arms folded and with an air of polite expectancy.

If he hoped by this to discompose her, she fumed inwardly, he would soon discover his mistake. Nothing was more guaranteed to put her on her mettle. She had known from the first that she could outsing and outplay the exquisite Lady Arabella, fine though she undoubtedly was, but until this moment she had no desire to prove it. Now she discarded the bright little ditty she had intended to perform and sat for a moment calming her thoughts.

The Handel aria that she chose had been her grandfather's favorite, and perhaps because of this her voice that evening possessed an added quality of depth and purity that reduced her audience to rapt silence. As the last notes died away, she sat with her hands resting lightly on the keys, her head bowed to mask the extent to which she herself had been moved by the experience.

When the applause came, accompanied by cries for more, she declined with an abruptness quite out of character for her and stood up. The long windows close by were wide open to the terrace beyond, and she slipped through them before they could besiege her further.

The sound of voices grew faint. The night air was balmy, the stars sharp and clear in a velvet sky, but as Perdita walked quickly along the terrace, she was aware of nothing beyond the hollowing of pain within her. It was some weeks since she had felt Sir Edwin's loss with so much raw anguish, but Handel's "Care Selve" had brought him back to her in a particularly vivid way. She leaned against the balustrade, her arms wrapped about her for comfort.

St. Ive had followed her out, and stood for a few moments—intrigued by the utter stillness of the lone slight figure ahead of him outlined against the night sky. Slowly, he moved forward.

"Are you all right, Miss Grant?"

She turned her head reluctantly at the sound of his voice, and the lights from the house picked up the sheen of tears gilding her cheeks.

"Yes, of course."

The unaccustomed huskiness in the brief utterance moved him strangely. He turned and leaned on the balustrade beside her, looking out over the shadowed gardens.

"You have a remarkable voice," he said quietly, not looking at her. "It should be heard more often." She made a self-depreciating gesture that prompted him to add, "That aria meant something special to you, I think?"

She let out a long shuddering sigh. "I should have known better than to attempt it, and am well served for wishing to show off!" She shook her head at his murmured objection to this. "Isn't it odd that music can evoke memories and emotions in a way that mere words can never do? My grandfather taught me 'Care Selve' when I was a girl—I haven't sung it since his death, and I felt his presence so strongly in that room just now that I expected to look up and see him sitting there, the slight movement of his hand marking time as he was used to do." She attemped a smile. "Which is highly fanciful, not to say absurd, looked at rationally!"

"One should never seek to rationalize emotions, Miss Grant," he said calmly. "Like dreams, they seldom survive the cold light of reason."

Perdita gave a hiccuping little laugh, thankful for once for his clear incisive manner. She fumbled in her reticule for a handkerchief. "There speaks the cynic, sir."

"Not at all. A cynic would not admit the reality of the emotions in the first place."

Her laugh this time was less tremulous, more appreciative. "Thank you. I feel much restored already. I do so dislike people who indulge in mawkish sentimentality!"

"You are being neither, I promise you. Simply human."

She was dabbing ineffectively at her eyes, and without another word he took the scrap of lacy cambric from her and wiped away the tears with infinite care, continuing to stare down into her upturned face long after he had finished.

Darkness blurred the harder stronger edges of his face, lending it instead a kind of brooding mystery that held a strange excitement. She felt herself swaying toward him as though compelled by a force beyond her control, and as she did so he cupped her face in his hands and bent to close each eyelid with a feather-light kiss. Then his mouth was on hers.

"Piers? Are you there?"

Lady Arabella's voice, full of dagger-sharp edges, came from the open window. The mood was broken instantly, and he straightened up. Perdita thought she heard him swear softly.

"You go along in," she said with amazing poise. "I need another moment or two to compose myself."

When she did return, all trace of her distress had gone and she was able to withstand all the questions and the praise heaped upon her with equanimity. The four older members of the party were about to play a few hands of whist, while the others continued to talk.

"Shall you hunt this winter, Miss Grant?" asked Sir James. "I have not forgotten how well you acquitted yourself at Melton—two years ago, was it, that we met?"

"At Lord Rackham's," she said with a sigh. "Pray do not remind me, sir! I very much fear that I shall be obliged to forgo the pleasure this year."

"Oh, surely not! I am not generally in favor of ladies in the hunting field, but for you, ma'am, I would willingly make an exception anytime!" He looked around him with a wheezing laugh. "One of the few ladies with the skill to outride most gentlemen in the field!"

"I can vouch for that," said the duke without raising his eyes from the cards.

"Indeed?" Lady Arabella's voice was all sweetness. "How very . . . enterprising of you, Miss Grant! It has always seemed to me such an energetic pastime. Do you not end up all covered in mud?"

"Frequently," Perdita said cordially. "But that is a small price to pay for the invigorating sensation of well-being that one enjoys, and the mud soon washes off."

"Well said, ma'am." Sir James was growing more enthusiastic by the minute. "Why, I well remember—"

"My love!" murmured his wife in quiet exasperation.

"What? Oh, yes—quite so, m'dear." He smiled sheepishly. "Get me started and I'll bore on for hours, as my poor Clara knows to her cost." He patted his wife's hand. "All horses, hounds, and hunting, what?"

Perdita chuckled. "Well, it *is* tempting—especially if one has had a particularly good run! But I mustn't dwell on the prospect too much or I shall grow maudlin."

"But how is this, Miss Grant?" put in Lord Lyndon. "It seems a great pity if you must forgo something from which you obviously derive so much enjoyment."

"Oh, it is very fine for you gentlemen, my lord! You are not governed by the proprieties as we are. And even were my circumstances otherwise, I am not sure whether my hunter will be sufficiently recovered."

The duke glanced up. "Is our beloved Satan out of sorts, then?"

Perdita quite failed to hide her surprise. "Why—yes. He was badly cut yesterday as we were riding home." She looked across instinctively to Lord St.

Ive and was in time to see a fleeting expression of annoyance cross his face. "But I thought . . ."

His slight shrug conveyed little. "I saw no point in troubling my father needlessly. All that could have been done was done."

Freddie Ponsford was also watching his friend in a puzzled way, but thought better of adding to his discomfort. Ivo had ever been a law unto himself.

The duke's expression was unreadable, though Perdita had a feeling that he would not be content to leave matters as they were. No doubt explanations would be demanded later. She had no idea why St. Ive hadn't told his father about the accident, but the change in his manner toward her this evening, inexplicable as it was, prompted her to say something by way of mitigation.

"Lord St. Ive has been more than kind," she said, very conscious of his eyes upon her. "His groom is already performing wonders, and has quite won George over! But I fear it will be some considerable time before Satan is able to gallop over Claverton Down again, and that I am going to miss quite abominably!"

The duke studied her face for a moment in silence. Then he returned his attention to the card table as if to signify that the matter was closed, and the conversation moved on to other things.

It was only later, going home in the carriage, that Perdita again fell to wondering why the marquis had been so secretive about the accident. He really was the oddest man. Every time she thought she had his measure, he did something new to confound her. Miss Midgely had enjoyed her evening enormously and was more talkative than usual, so that she hardly noticed how quiet her companion had grown.

THE DUKE OF ANDERLEY had also enjoyed his evening. Only one thing had marred it. As he limped from the room on his way to bed, he turned and fixed his son with an uncompromising gaze.

"Piers, be so good as to accompany me, if you please. There is a small matter upon which I would value your opinion." And so that there could be no doubt of his intention, added softly, "It is a matter of some urgency."

Chapter 14

*H*ARRY AND AMARYLLIS had come home briefly from London before going up to Warwickshire to spend August with Amaryllis's mother. It was duty rather than pleasure for Harry, who found his mother-in-law a sore trial.

"No matter how I put myself about for her, she manages to make me feel inadequate! Know what I mean?"

Perdita laughed. She had met Amaryllis's mama only once, and had found her to be a restless ambitious woman, forever complaining, and so protective of her one and only daughter that it was probable that she had still not forgiven Harry for robbing her of the cache of being able to claim a marquis for a son-in-law.

"By the bye," he said, "your cousin hasn't been here inflicting himself on you again, has he?"

"No." Perdita felt a slight sinking of the heart. "Never tell me he's purse-pinched again? I thought you said he had won a fortune or somesuch."

"Well, not a fortune, precisely—and what there was would probably have burned a hole in his pocket until he'd wagered it all to perdition again, though I've no way of knowing *that*." Harry grinned at her horrified face. "No need to get yourself in a pucker! I wouldn't have mentioned the fellow, except that I saw him not two days since."

"Here?" Perdita exclaimed.

"Well, not in Bath precisely. I'd been over to Charlcombe and was riding back when a Stanhope passed me. I only had a glimpse, but the driver did look remarkably like Tillot."

"If Bertram was driving a Stanhope, he must be well in funds," Perdita said. "In which case he would be unlikely to seek me out. Even so, I do hope you were mistaken."

She asked Mrs. Windlesham when they met in Milson Street, where the latter had been purchasing some new ribbons to trim one of Clarissa's bonnets. "Only think, my love, that new woman, Mrs. Gay, is charging threepence for the paltriest of satin! If they had not been exactly the colors I was wanting, I declare I would have left the counter. But you may be sure I let her know how absurdly expensive I thought them."

Perdita hid a smile, knowing full well that it was a point of honor with her old friend to complain about prices. She deftly changed the subject and was considerably reassured to learn that Mrs. Windlesham had no knowledge of Mr. Tillot's having returned to Bath, "and even if it had escaped my notice, you may be sure Mr. Windlesham would have heard of it, and would have mentioned it to me."

From here her grasshopper mind turned to the duke's party yet again, though she had thoroughly dissected it on the morning after when she had called upon Perdita.

"Are Lord St. Ive's guests still at the Court, do you know? We still talk about the evening, so very pleasant as it was—and everyone so friendly."

Perdita thought of the way Lady Arabella had

slighted Mrs. Windlesham and could only be thankful that she had not been aware of it.

"I believe Sir James and his wife have now gone, and the Lyndons, but Lady Arabella is still there—and Mr. Ponsford, though I doubt her ladyship will remain much longer. She finds the country very slow, I think."

"Ah," said Mrs. Windlesham with an arch smile. "But we all know *why* she stays, do we not? And so long as Lord St. Ive feels it to be his duty to support his papa, she will, I am sure, not find life wholly unsupportable!"

Her presence did, however, diminish Perdita's pleasures somewhat. Satan's incapacity was an added blow—and meant that she must either drive to the Court in the gig, or walk through the woods, taking the path she used to frequent with Satan—a not unpleasurable pastime on a fine summer's day—or forgo her visits altogether.

In the event she compromised, going less often and reluctantly deciding to use the gig. She had walked a couple of times but had felt inexplicably nervous as she had never done on horseback—every unexplainable rustle in the undergrowth seemed to have a sinister cause. It was that absurd accident, she told herself, angry that she should have permitted it to affect her so. And when on the second occasion she had walked someone had fired off a shotgun close by her, making her jump almost out of her skin, she decided that the gig would be less nerve-racking.

She had, upon reaching the Court, mentioned the incident to the marquis, but though he said little, she was left with the distinct impression that he thought she was simply starting at shadows.

And he could be right, she told herself mockingly. But the feeling remained, and she resolved to be watchful.

However, her situation was to improve in a totally unexpected way when the duke came to see her, driving in an open landau—and trotting alongside, ridden by a groom, was a beautifully behaved bay mare, full of go, if Perdita was any judge.

"Why, what is this, sir?" she exclaimed, coming forward to run an appreciative hand down its neck.

"I thought you might appreciate the loan of a prime little goer to tide you over until Satan is fully fit."

"Oh, my dear sir, what can I say? 'Thank you' seems so inadequate."

The duke's eyes glinted. "Your obvious pleasure is all the thanks I require. It occurred to me that I had a dozen or more horses eating their heads off in my Warwickshire stables. What simpler than to send Maxwell along there to bring one back. You will have the satisfaction of knowing that you are keeping at least one of them exercised."

"I shall take the greatest care of her," Perdita said with enthusiasm. "What is her name?"

The duke regarded the animal with careless affection. "She answers to Lady. I think you will find her well mannered—and she's a good little goer and jumps strongly off her hocks, should you wish to hunt her."

"Oh, but I am hoping that Satan will be fit again by the winter."

"Doing well, is he?"

"Far better than I had dared to hope, thanks to Lord St. Ive's groom. If you would care to drive around to the stable, you may judge for yourself and we shall see how he takes to his new stable companion."

The mare settled down at once, her temperament being both lively and tractable. She had not been accustomed to carrying a lady, his grace told Perdita, but she took to it as agreeably as she did all else, and Perdita was overjoyed to be able to resume her early-morning rides. She had always, for propriety's sake, taken the undergroom along, though at that hour they seldom met anyone else, and he was invariably left well behind when she gave herself up to a good invigorating gallop.

On the second morning after Lady's arrival, when she had taken her up to Lansdown to try out her paces, Perdita was surprised to find that she had company. She was even more surprised to discover who her fellow rider was.

"Good morning, Miss Grant," said Lord St. Ive, reining in and raising his hat to her. Seeing her expression, he added imperturbably, "You mentioned the other evening that this was one of your favorite haunts."

Perdita regarded him suspiciously. "If you have come to brangle . . ."

"Why ever should you think that?"

"How should I know? Except that you seldom seek me out unless it is to provoke a quarrel—indeed, it has been your avowed intention from the first to oppose me at every turn." She threw back her head to challenge him, eye to eye. "But if you mean to cut up stiff about my accepting your father's kind offer to loan me this beauty . . ." She ran a gauntleted hand down the mare's neck, to the animal's obvious pleasure.

St. Ive gave her back a bland look. "Such a thought never entered my head."

"It didn't?" Her suspicions, far from being allayed, were fueled even more. "Then why are you here?"

"Must I have a reason?" He shrugged. "Then let us say that I thought you might like some company for a change."

"How noble of you. But I quite enjoy my solitary rides."

The look he gave her was decidedly quizzical. "Now who is being provoking, my girl? But it won't wash. I am resolved to be agreeable whatever the cost. Shall we proceed?" They turned together and put the horses to an easy trot.

Perdita bit her lip, not knowing what to make of him in this mood. "About your father—" she began, but he would have none of it.

"No, don't tell me," he said. "I see now that I had quite the wrong idea about you, and consequently I withdraw all my objections and wish you happy. I am told that May marrying December often works out remarkably well."

"Oh, but . . ." How could he be so vexatious!

"Tell me, have you tried that mare out over a testing gallop yet?" he inquired amiably. "If not, this would be an excellent place to put her through her paces."

By now thoroughly exasperated with him, without quite knowing why she should be when he was being so obliging, she let the mare out, calling over her shoulder, "Very well, my lord, I will race you to that clump of elms ahead," and, unrepentant about having taken unfair advantage, she urged Lady onward, delighted by the way she flew over the ground. In the end she won by a nose, and reined in, breathless but triumphant, her spirits fully restored and her cheeks aglow.

"Very well, madam, I'll give you that, but next time beware! There'll be no quarter given then."

"Pooh!" she laughed back at him. "As if I should need or expect it."

St. Ive found himself prey to an overwhelming desire to lift her from the saddle and kiss her while she had no breath to resist him, and cursed himself for a damned fool for not doing so. But something of the force at work in him was mirrored in his eyes, and Perdita felt its impact. It aroused an answering chord of—fear?—panic? She could not give it a name, but it was not the first time that he had made her feel that way.

"I must be getting back," she said.

"Of course," he said mockingly. "It must be all of half past seven."

"Yes, but poor Tom is kicking his heels there," she insisted, indicating the distant figure of the young groom sitting a little glumly on the elderly roan cob.

"Ah," he said, and the sound was invested with all kinds of meaning.

They turned and began to ride back at a decorous trot. Perdita was suddenly aware of how beautiful the morning was—the blue sky still translucently pink on the horizon, the air crisp and clear.

"You have always lived in Bath, I take it?" said his lordship.

"Yes. Since I was four. My parents were killed in an accident, and I came to live at Marston Grange with my grandfather."

He gave her a sideways look. "It's not exactly a mecca of high living. Don't you find it damnably flat?"

"I have never done so in the past," she said defensively. "But then I went about a great deal with Grandpa. He had a great many interesting friends, so we were seldom dull."

"A giddy round of dissipation, in fact," he mused laconically. "I begin to see now."

"See what, my lord?" she demanded, stung by his tone.

"How you came to regard my father, who whatever else he may be knows how to make a woman feel like a woman, as some kind of knight in shining armor," he returned. "Were there no young men to sweep you off your feet?"

"Plenty," she said angrily. "But I found them in the main to be arrogant, opinionated, or simply tedious! Give me one good reason why I should have exchanged the company of an intelligent man like my grandfather for someone who merely wants a woman to run his household and bear his children, and whose conversation seldom rises above the banal?"

"You seem to have been singularly unfortunate in the young men with whom you have become acquainted," said St. Ive drolly.

"Perhaps so," she agreed grudgingly.

He appeared to be measuring his words. "But suddenly things have changed. Your grandfather is gone, and your girlhood is past. Small wonder that you should turn to my father. He can give you all that you think you want—the maturity of your grandfather, the allure of a certain worldly courtesy, and, most of all, an acceptable escape from those long years of spinsterhood that stretch ahead."

Perdita could hardly believe what she was hearing, the cutting irony, the arrogant assumptions. It was several moments before she could conquer her indignation sufficiently to speak.

"Forgive me, my lord, but I am growing a little tired of being told that I am at my last prayers! You are the second man within the space of a week to assume that I will be grateful to any man who offers me marriage in order to escape the stigma of dwindling into spinsterhood." Her eyes clashed with his. "For my part, I fail to see what is so very dreadful about remaining unwed. In fact, there are times such as now when the prospect has enormous appeal, and I find myself with a positive yearning to court notoriety by becoming an eccentric like Lady Hester Stanhope."

To her astonishment and mortification he gave a great shout of laughter. "Oh, that is much better! I

like you in this mood. But you said I was the
second man to make assumptions about you. Who
was the first?"

Perdita's eyes kindled, remembering. "Who else
but our esteemed clergyman, who thought my liai-
son with his grace so little short of indecent that
he felt compelled to make an honest woman of
me—a decision, I felt, that was not uninfluenced
by the comfortable competence I should bring with
me!" She broke off, appalled by her indiscretion.

The marquis said with a quiver in his voice,
"That pompous windbag Gilles actually proposed
to you?"

"Yes," she admitted, scarlet-faced. "But I should
not have told you. It was an unforgivable betrayal
of confidence, and I must beg that you will let it go
no further. You see how my tongue runs away
with me when I am out of reason cross!" She drew
a deep breath. "And I don't know why it should be
that you seem to bring out the very worst in me!"

"Don't you?" His eyes narrowed to bright slits.

"No," she said resolutely, "unless it is your capacity for being contentious. But I am quite done
with you now, my lord, except to say that I do not,
contrary to your assumption, view your father in
any roseate glow—I have on many occasions during the past months been on the receiving end of
his less endearing traits, for he was, when in pain,
frequently ill-tempered, almost impossible to please,
and every bit as cuttingly sarcastic as you at your
worst." She saw his eyebrows shoot up and concluded with a final thrust, "But never once during
our acquaintance has he talked down to me, or
made me feel like one of those pitiable women who
have only two main functions in life—neither of
which requires either brain or wit! And if he should
do me the honor of offering for me, my acceptance
would not be for any of the reasons you so glibly
advanced!"

"I see." They were almost the last words he uttered for the remainder of the journey, but they were by then so close to home that she was able with some relief to bid him goodbye. He replied with a brevity that verged upon curtness, and rode quickly away.

Perdita had ample time to reflect upon her behavior, and each time she reviewed it, it seemed more discreditable than the last. How could she have ripped up at him in that rag-mannered way? The fact that he had asked for trouble was little consolation. What had become of the happy, good-humored creature that she had always thought herself to be?

Miss Midgely was wondering rather the same thing. Not that Perdita was crabby—simply much quieter than was usual in her. Several times she was on the verge of broaching her concern, but each time something in Perdita's eyes stopped her. So she remained what she always was, patient, watchful, and ready to be of help if and when required to be so.

IT WAS WITH A VERY real reluctance that Perdita visited Anderley Court the following day. Freddie Ponsford, her last buffer between herself and the marquis, had left that morning to visit a friend who owned one of the finest grouse shoots in Yorkshire—and that left only Lady Arabella. Perdita was surprised that she had stuck it out so long. Perhaps her feelings for St. Ive went deeper than would appear to be the case, for though she made no secret of her impatience to be gone from Anderley, she clearly had no intention of leaving without him.

To her immense relief, however, she arrived to find his grace alone in the garden room.

"Reprieve at last," he informed her with an exaggerated sigh. "Milady received word yesterday from friends living not twenty miles from here, begging her to go and stay for as long as she pleased. When Piers agreed to take her, she could scarcely stay to pack her trunks! Do you not notice a change in the atmosphere, my dear?"

"For shame, sir!" She laughed. "I thought you would take pleasure from having a diamond of the first water like Lady Arabella to grace your house."

The duke lifted a disparaging eyebrow. "Diamonds of the first water may have a brilliance desirable to the beholder, but they can also be hard, cold, and damnably expensive!" He patted her hand. "I would rather have my pearl of great price any day."

He felt the involuntary tenseness his gesture provoked and looked more closely at her. "Is something wrong?"

"No, of course not," she said quickly—too quickly.

" 'No, of course not,' " he mocked her gently. "Come now, my dear, you have never dissembled with me in the past. What has happened to make you do so now?"

Perdita stood up and moved restlessly away from him. "Nothing, except . . . It isn't easy to know how to explain without unwittingly giving offense."

The duke watched the myriad expressions chasing across her face. He said with a certain wryness, "Then suppose I put it into words for you?"

She glanced quickly at him.

"I am not blind, my dear Perdita. Nor am I a fool. You are troubled lest I might be taking too seriously the small fiction we concocted between us for Piers's benefit. Am I close?"

She came swiftly back to sit beside him. "I am *very* fond of you. . . ."

He grimaced ruefully. "That, my child, is the kiss of death to any suitor's aspiration!" She opened her mouth to rephrase her explanation, but he put up an elegant hand. "No, pray don't attempt to qualify the nature of your feelings for me. I assure you it is quite unnecessary for you to do so. Our little deception has been harmless—and has not, I think, gone beyond these walls, though no doubt your frequent visits have set a few tongues clacking." He smiled faintly. "I may say that were I twenty years younger, the outcome would be very different, but then the situation would not have arisen in the first place."

"No." Her own smile combined amusement with relief. "I'm not sure whether I'm glad or sorry."

He carried her hand to his lips. "I shall take that as a compliment, whether or not it was so intended. I make but one condition."

Perdita's candid gray eyes widened a little.

"That you will continue to visit me," he said.

"Gladly, sir." She rose to leave, her smile now frankly teasing. "To stop now would be far more likely to give rise to speculation!"

He laughed softly. When she had almost reached the door he called after her. She turned to look back at him.

"Would you like me to tell Piers of our changed circumstances when he returns?"

She put up her chin and with the utmost dignity said, "What you choose to tell your son can be of no possible interest to me, your grace." But her flaming face told quite another story.

His soft laughter followed her mockingly out of the door.

Chapter 15

THE AFTERNOON WAS WARM, even by the standards of early August, but the weather was not the sole cause of the high color in Perdita's cheeks. If she went home directly, Midge would surely remark upon it, and she could not be certain of fending her off with any degree of conviction.

With this thought in mind she cut across the parkland and cantered along under the trees that skirted the row of workers' cottages. Here a small stream ran, and the happy combination of water and shade produced a pleasant cooling waft of air. The women sitting outside their doors answered her greetings with broad smiles, aware how much they owed her for their improved conditions.

Perdita deliberately emptied her mind of all the confused embarrassing thoughts that had pursued her from the Court, the inference that the duke had drawn from her wish to end that silly charade, which had made her feel like a gauche schoolgirl. She consoled herself that with any luck, St. Ive would remain wherever it was he had gone with Lady Arabella for a very long time, and then return immediately to London, his father by now being so much recovered. In fact, she would not be at all surprised to learn before long that his grace too would be off to more exciting places. The shooting season would soon be in full swing, and he would be sure to receive any number of invitations. Just for a moment pangs of jealousy consumed her, but she fought them off and resolutely gave her thoughts a happier direction.

Finally she felt sufficiently calm to make her way home, and she set off back across the parkland with Lady at a brisk canter. They had crossed the drive and were heading for the shelter of the woods when Perdita felt the saddle give with a kind of jolt and begin to slide. It happened so quickly that she had lost her balance and was falling before she could even free her foot from the stirrup. Lady, in full canter, was clearly frightened, and in the absence of any comforting presence to guide her, she increased her stride, dragging Perdita along in her wake.

It seemed as though she bumped along through the undergrowth forever before the mare responded to her calls and slowed down, though it was but a matter of moments. She kicked her foot free, just as, with a wrenching sound, the saddle, already hanging at a ludicrous angle under the mare's belly, gave way and crashed to the ground, causing Lady to shy violently.

For some time Perdita lay winded and feeling bruised and battered in every inch of her body, her left knee aching abominably. Then very gingerly she moved her limbs experimentally one by one before easing herself across to where the saddle lay. She pulled back the flap to expose the girth leathers and saw at once what had happened. Her blood ran cold as she visualized what her fate might have been had she been going at a full gallop.

It was as she was on the point of attempting to

get to her feet that a twig snapped nearby. She froze, waiting in an unnatural silence—for what, she was not sure. But it came at last—a distinct rustling in the undergrowth. With her heart beating so loudly that she was sure it must be heard for miles, she lowered herself carefully back to the ground and lay quite still, her hands pushed into the pockets of her skirt.

The rustling took on the character of footsteps coming nearer. It might be one of the duke's deer, Perdita reasoned, but without conviction, for they would never in her experience come beyond scenting distance of a human. As the footsteps came nearer she held her breath and watched through slitted eyes as a pair of legs came into view, coarse breeches stuffed into ill-fitting boots. They stopped beside her, and she sensed rather than saw the man bend to look down at her. Then he stepped past her and reached for the saddle.

Perdita sat up, scarcely aware of her quietly screaming limbs, and said in a voice that was remarkably steady, "Yes, do please pick it up, there's a good fellow. It is much too heavy for me to carry all the way back to the Court."

He spun around clumsily, a muttered oath beneath his breath, his mouth hanging ludicrously open. He was slight, little more than a boy really, with gypsy-dark hair and eyes that were cunning rather than intelligent. And she knew him. He was a recent addition to the duke's stables, taken on at St. Ive's suggestion, to cope with all the extra work.

She took advantage of that moment of shock to get to her feet, and as she did so, his eyes were flicking about him, weighing his next move.

"Don't," she advised him crisply.

He looked her over and must have been encouraged by what he saw, for the beginnings of a leary grin distorted his mouth. "You ain't exactly in any case to be tellin' me what to do, lady! Why, I bet if I was to nudge you wiv my little finger, 'ere, you'd keel over like ninepins!"

"Yes, but you won't do anything of the kind, my lad," she said, withdrawing her hand from her pocket. He sucked in his breath as he found himself staring down the barrel of Sir Edwin's pistol, which she had recently taken to carrying with her as a precaution. "What you will do," she continued in a voice that brooked no argument, "is to pick up that saddle and walk ahead of me. Do you understand?"

He shrugged.

"What is your name?"

He glowered at her. "Ain't sayin'."

She sighed. "As you please. But lest you should harbor any doubt as to my ability to use this weapon, I give you fair warning that I have been able to shoot with commendable accuracy since I was a girl."

He mouthed a string of scurrilous abuse at her, much of which cast considerable doubt upon her parentage, but when he saw that this left her unmoved, he reluctantly did as he was bade, while she limped behind him with the mare's rein looped over her arm. She realized suddenly that she must have lost her hat in the fall, and that her hair was probably in disarray and harboring bits of grass and twig, but it seemed relatively unimportant when compared with all else.

There were moments during that interminable walk when only sheer determination kept Perdita going—moments when her mind wandered into the fastness of memory, conjuring up all those odd disturbing incidents that had so plagued her recently—Satan's accident that was no accident, the unaccountable shot when she was riding in the woods, the constant feeling that she was being watched. She had little doubt now that the lad trudging so truculently ahead of her was responsible for it all, but at whose instigation?

And then, as her painful limping gait took on a curious uneven kind of march rhythm, it seemed to form a pattern of words. *The marquis hired him, the marquis hired him*, they went on repeating themselves until they beat in her brain. The pistol was becoming heavier by the minute. Several times her arm dropped lower and lower, but each time she recovered and leveled it with renewed determination.

At first, when she heard her name called, she thought that particular voice was all part of her private fantasy.

"*Miss Grant*! Perdita, in God's name, what is going on?"

She looked up into St. Ive's face. It was blank with shock . . . or guilt? She had no power to stop the thought. How forbidding his face was. He was asking her for the pistol, but she fended him off, her fingers still firmly on the trigger.

"Give it to me, Perdita," he said quietly. "You haven't cocked it, so you can hardly hope to do much good with it."

She looked at the pistol dully and saw that he was right. Suddenly it didn't seem to matter anymore. She handed it to him without a word and stood, immobile, unsure what to do next, quite unaware of the profound effect her disheveled appearance was having upon him.

The stable lad, however, was in no doubt about what he should do. Taking advantage of the marquis's intervention, he dropped the saddle and took to his heels. But he didn't get far before St. Ive's voice reached him, harsh with reality.

"Stop—or by God *I'll* do it for you!"

He ducked low and began to run in a desperate zigzagging gait. A moment later there was a deafening explosion, and a searing pain in his thigh sent him sprawling to the ground, sobbing and clutching at his leg.

The sound of the shot brought Perdita to her senses. She looked with horror at the smoking pistol in St. Ive's hand. "What have you done?" she said.

"I'm hoping that you will tell me," replied his lordship. "You were the one who had the boy at pistol point." He saw that she was swaying and had an arm about her immediately.

"You could have killed him," said Perdita faintly.

"I could have," he admitted. "But only if I had meant to do so."

He looked down at her intently. "Do you feel up to telling me what all this is about?"

She stared resolutely at the diamond pin winking in his cravat. "I thought you might be able to tell me," she said, her voice subdued.

"What kind of an answer is that, for God's sake?"

Perdita couldn't be more specific. The words refused to come. The feel of his arms about her, his very closeness, was robbing her of all coherent thought. She tried to move away, but at once her knee protested and she was obliging to bite back a gasp of pain. His hold tightened. His voice was almost vicious.

"Don't be a fool!"

"Is that what I am?" she said on a sob. "Yes, perhaps you're right." She shook her head wearily and indicated the saddle lying discarded in the grass. "And perhaps *you* should take a look at that." As he frowned and hesitated, she added with a kind of bitter flippancy, "You needn't worry. I'm hardly in any condition to run away!"

The expression in his eyes almost frightened

her. But after a a moment he removed his arm
from her and strode swiftly away. Left unsupported,
Perdita almost fell, but a soft whinny reminded her
of Lady's presence. The mare nudged her gently in
the back, and with a relieved sigh she leaned her
weight against the solid bulk of Lady's shoulder.
Nearby the stable boy had taken the none too clean
handkerchief from around his neck and now sat
frantically attempting to tie it around his leg.

"Are you all right?"

Her concern met with oaths. "Do I look all right?
Bleedin' 'alf to death, I am!" But his eyes kept
flicking fearfully toward the marquis.

It took St. Ive no more than a moment to find
the torn girth leathers. He looked closer, no, not
torn—each one had been cunningly cut through
almost all the way, leaving the additional strain put
on them to complete the illusion that they had
split, and if the rider had been going at speed . . .

In mounting anger he realized that this was no
mere prank, no attempt to frighten, but a cold-
blooded attempt at murder! He stood up and through
a red mist of rage saw the stable boy dragging
himself toward the shelter of the woods in a feeble
attempt to hide.

In a moment he had caught up with him and
had him by the scruff of the neck, deaf to his
terrified howls, deaf and blind to everything but a
determination to shake the truth out of him.

"I don't know nuffing! God's strewth, I don't! I
just did what I was told . . . A-ah!"

"Told by whom? Ten seconds, you miserable
little toad, and then I snap your neck in two!"

"*Stop it!* Stop it at once, do you hear me?"

It was Perdita's voice, sharp with anger and fear.
She had seen the boy dangling helplessly from St.
Ive's grasp, and it truly seemed that any moment
might be his last. Clinging to Lady's rein, she

hobbled across to them and was appalled to see
that the attempted bandage had been quite inef-
fective and that the blood was flowing afresh from
the jagged rent in the boy's breeches. Close to, she
could almost feel the violence emanating from the
marquis, and it was indeed frightening.

"My lord, you must not harm him further! Truly
you must not!"

St. Ive's hold slackened, and the lad slumped to
the ground with great sobbing gasps. He watched
him in disgust for a moment and then turned his
anger on Perdita. "He was ripe to tell me—or don't
you want to know who tried to kill you?"

Did she? She said dully, "You can talk to him
later—when his wound has been properly attended
to."

His narrowed eyes still glittered, but now there
was a twist of arid amusement about his mouth.
"Perdita Grant—who but you would be so eager to
give succor to your would-be assassin?"

"We don't know that for sure," she said quickly.

"We know."

"Well, anyway, I certainly have no wish to see
him suffer unnecessarily," she insisted. "Though
how are we to get him back to the house? Clearly
he can't walk."

"Perhaps," he suggested with deep irony, "you
would like me to carry him?"

"Don't be silly," she said absently. "I was wondering if it might be possible for him to ride Lady—if
you would help him up." While he continued to
look at her in disbelief, she turned to the boy, who
had been listening with the beginning of hope. "I
still don't know your name."

"Jem, miss," he mumbled.

"Well, Jem, do you think you *could* ride?"

The genuine concern in her voice gave him a
queer sort of feeling. She must surely be touched

in the attic to be worritin' about the likes of him! Still . . . "Course I can, miss," he said eagerly, the burning pain in his leg for the moment taking precedence over his fear of the marquis, and thoughts of what might happen to him later.

"Well, then?" She glanced at St. Ive, who shot her a look of exasperation before lifting the boy not ungently and setting him on Lady's back.

"Fine. And what am I to do with you, Miss Grant?" he asked with exaggerated solicitude. "Throw you over my shoulder? Pray don't hesitate to make whatever use of me you may wish!"

She flushed. A little while ago he had called her Perdita. She said stiffly, "Oh, I shall do very well if you will give me your arm."

"Not true," he said with soft vehemence. "You can hardly walk."

"Of course I can," she lied valiantly. "I simply twisted my knee slightly when my foot got caught in the stirrup, and it aches a little, but I expect the walk will do it good."

She avoided the compelling interrogation in his eyes, and to her relief he made no attempt to argue further.

Nevertheless, in spite of all her vainglory, Perdita was profoundly thankful to reach the house. The marquis left her in the garden while he went in search of Pendlebury and arranged for someone to take Jem in charge and keep him securely contained.

The duke had retired to his own rooms, much to her relief, for she had no wish to enter into tedious explanations. She was able to lie back in a comfortable chair listening to the soft splash of water while the majority of her bumps and bruises subsided to a dull ache and only her knee still throbbed with any degree of intensity. There were unpleasant questions to be answered, but she refused to confront them now. The tangy smell of the greenery that she loved wafted pleasantly across her senses, and her eyelids began to droop.

The marquis, coming in silently, watched her for a moment in frowning thought. Her disordered hair had drifted across her face and clung to the chairback like strands of spun silver; there were deep shadows beneath her eyes and lines of pain starkly etched about her mouth, while her body, so innately graceful, slumped in an attitude of utter weariness. She looked in that moment utterly defenseless, and he found himself prey to an overwhelming intensity of emotion that shook him to his soul and left him unsure whether he wanted to shake her for being so incredibly obstinate, or kiss her and go on kissing her until she promised to stay with him forever.

As though summoned by the sheer force of his emotions, Perdita stirred and opened her eyes to find him staring intimidatingly down his nose at her, his whole expression uncompromisingly severe. She knew she ought to sit up, but a curious lethargy held her inert, oblivious of the effect she was having upon him.

"The duke told me that you had gone away," she said inconsequentially.

"I had, but I came back. And as well for you that I did, don't you think?"

Unsure how to answer, she resorted to a poor attempt at flippancy. "Well, *I* certainly couldn't have got Jem up onto Lady's back. On the other hand, the need might never have arisen, since it was you who put the bullet in him! In fact, now I think about it, I was managing rather well until you came!"

"You were all but dead on your feet and probably *would* be dead by now at the hands of that little toad," he said savagely. "So don't flim-flam me with feeble jokes!" The violence of his reaction made her flinch. He set one hand either side of her head on the chairback and bent close so that she was forced to press back, squinting inelegantly into his blazing eyes. "What exactly did you mean when you suggested that I might know about the attempt on your life?"

His anger brought out a sudden spurt of spirit. "It just seems a little odd that I was never prone to accidents until you came along."

For a moment she thought he would strike her. Then abruptly he stood up and flung away, running a hand distractedly through his hair. Finally he came back to say with a kind of hurt vehemence, "Do you really imagine for one moment that I would—*could* ever do such a thing to you?" And absurdly, she wanted to cry—to take him in her arms and assure him that she had never thought anything of the kind.

She could hardly speak for the lump in her throat. "You made no secret of your determination to get me out of your father's life, right from that first day."

"But . . . good God, girl! A clash of wills, however violent, is not an inducement to murder! If that is *really* what you think—"

"No, of course I don't!" she exclaimed in a stifled voice, and then, at the full realization of the extent to which her own feelings for him had changed, and fearful of betraying those feelings, she panicked and attempted to rise, intent only upon getting away before she made a complete fool of herself. Her knee would not bear her weight, and she sank with a groan.

The marquis swore viciously. "Fool that I am, I should never have let you walk on it! Which knee is it? Show me," he said peremptorily, and as her eyes widened with comprehension and he saw the refusal already forming on her lips, "Oh, good God, this is no time to be missish! If I don't take a look at it, how can I possibly do anything about it?"

"It doesn't matter," she muttered, scarlet-faced.

"Well, of course it matters! Look, my dear silly girl, think what you will of me, revile me if you must, but don't, I beg of you, insult my intelligence by treating me to a display of false heroics!"

"And d-don't you bully me, you abominable man!" she protested with appalling childishness. "I am *not* your girl—not a girl at all, in fact, as you were so obliging as to tell me!" And then the pain and the misery all became too much for her, and to her intense mortification she burst into tears.

"Oh, the devil take my damnable tongue! I didn't mean it! Dearest Perdita, please don't cry!" Hardly daring to believe the words she was hearing, Perdita was helpless to stop the tears once they had begun. And he, for fear of causing further hurt to her already painful knee, could only crouch beside her and take her hands in his, kissing them and begging her to forgive his stupidity.

Finally, in exasperation, he exclaimed, "Oh, dammit, this is ridiculous!"

And a cool suave voice from the doorway said, "I couldn't agree more, dear boy."

The duke had his quizzing glass up, and was surveying them with a disconcerting degree of interest.

Chapter 16

IT WAS A MOMENT of considerable delicacy. St. Ive stood up, adjusted the set of his coat, and felt distinctly at a disadvantage, a novel experience for him and one that he did not greatly care for. He met his father's eyes and found them less cold than he had expected—decidedly quizzical, in fact.

"Is that how you do it these days?" the duke queried lazily. "Egad, we had rather more finesse, I think!"

St. Ive flushed. "Sir," he began jerkily, "this must look quite unforgivable on my part, but if you would just grant me a few moments of your time— there are matters that I must explain—"

"The scene I witnessed a few moments ago surely was self-explanatory? Though I confess I had thought to see Perdita looking happier." He strolled forward to regard Perdita thoughtfully. She already had herself in hand and was blowing her nose in a fashion that brought a faint smile to his eyes. "My dear, since I would stake my life that I had not misread your feelings for my son, I can only infer you have not yet broken the news to him?"

She returned his smile a little tremulously, her pallor giving way to a suffusing wave of color. "No, sir."

"What news?" the marquis demanded sharply. "The devil! Will one of you tell me what is going on?"

His father was sanguine. "Perdita and I have agreed that we should not suit. In point of fact, I must confess we never had the least notion of doing so, though if my expectations are fulfilled, I have every hope of keeping her in the family."

"You mean the whole thing was a hum from the start?" St. Ive said angrily.

"Let us rather say that you jumped to the wrong conclusion and we did not go out of our way to disabuse you."

"Well, I call it a damnable trick to play! And as for your part in it—" He swung around on Perdita and saw that betraying tide of color. His anger evaportated on the instant, and he threw up his hands. "The only wonder is that you could ever learn to love such a blockhead!" He came closer, touched her face with gentle fingers. "You do love me, dearest girl? I think I could not bear it if you were still making game of me!"

"As if I would! Oh, my dear lord, I don't quite know how it has happened when we have been at daggers drawn almost from the first, but I have been finding of late that I am quite wretched when you are not near me."

Her declaration, delivered with a shy uncertainty that moved him deeply, was so revealing to him that he instinctively moved to take her in his arms, and only then remembered her injury.

"Oh, damn that knee of yours! I want to hold you—to kiss you! Only then shall I truly believe my incredible and undeserved good fortune!"

"Then hold me, dearest lord," she exclaimed. "I shall not regard a trifling pain in such a cause!"

St. Ive caught her up in his arms, lifting her almost clear of the ground as he held her close, breast to breast, and kissed her with a fierceness that left her breathless and glowing.

The duke observed their union with considerable satisfaction and moved to the door. "I am clearly *de trop*. I shall be in the library if and when you wish to talk."

It was some considerable time before either of them were sensible enough to face the more unpleasant side of the afternoon's events. But they did come down to earth at last. And then and only then did Perdita permit her lord to bind up her knee, which was stiff and swollen, enduring with fortitude a painful few minutes as he assured himself that nothing was broken, before applying to it a cold compress as advocated by the incomparable Septimus Goring.

"I fear it won't feel much better after all that mauling," St. Ive said sympathetically. "But if you rest it, and continue to apply the compresses, there should be a decided improvement soon. And I mean to be there to see that you do as you are told!"

"Odious man!" she exclaimed, by now resigned to her discomfort. "I hope you don't imagine that I am so besotted that I mean to let you ride roughshod over me!"

"On the contrary, I shall be the perfect lover and whisper a great deal of nonsense in your ear and feed you with kisses, so that you will have no possible excuse for coming to cuffs with me."

"I come to cuffs? Well, really!"

He closed her mouth with ruthless efficiency, and when she finally emerged from his embrace, she was disinclined to argue.

"There," he said. "You see how it is done!"

"Oh, it's easy enough to have your own way against a helpless female, but just wait until I am fully mobile."

He kissed her fingers one by one and said softly,

"You can have no idea how I look forward to it."
And then, with regret, "But for now, my dear love,
I think we had better go and tell my father all that
has happened. And then I shall take you home."

Miss Midgely was more shaken than she would
admit to see Perdita once more in distress, the
more so when the details were briefly explained to
her.

"But my dear, whoever would want to harm
you? I would vouch for it that you haven't an
enemy in the world!"

"Don't fuss, Midge dear," Perdita reassured her
with amazing cheerfulness, as Lord St. Ive carried
her up the stairs. "He is just overdramatizing the
whole thing." She wrinkled her nose at him. "And
no, sir, I will not be taken to my bed. I have spent
more time than enough recently incarcerated in
my room. You may take me to the drawing room, if
you please."

The tone of her voice drove all else from Miss
Midgely's mind. That, together with the happiness
shining out of Perdita's eyes, and the possessive
pride with which his lordship held her, could leave
little doubt in anyone's mind as to the change in
their relationship.

"So I am to wish you happy," she said with a
twinkle. "Well, I can't pretend that I am altogether
surprised."

"You aren't—" Perdita looked at her in astonishment. "Well, we were. Isn't that so, my lord?"

"That rather depends upon how totally honest
with myself I am," he admitted with a wry grin.

"Really?" She gazed at him, entranced. "You
mean all the time you were ripping up at me and
being quite horrid, you were . . ." Her eyes widened and she began to chuckle. "Oh, yes! I too!"

There was a little more of this foolishness with
everything on a lighthearted note, but when the

marquis came to leave, and Miss Midgely went downstairs with him, she thought he seemed preoccupied.

"Is everything all right, my lord?" she queried a little hesitantly, not wishing to seem presumptuous.

He turned to her, immediately apologetic. "Forgive me, ma'am, I didn't want to make an issue of it in Perdita's hearing. She may make light of her ordeal, but make no mistake, it was far from pleasant, and I don't want her troubled further." He looked keenly at Miss Midgely. "Can *you* think of anyone who would wish her harm?"

"To the extent of trying to kill her?" She quelled the ripple of apprehension and attacked the unpleasant possibility with her usual bluntness. "No, I can't. It was not mere sophistry on my part when I said she had not an enemy to her name. Oh, she has ruffled a few feathers here and there, but . . ." She met his look squarely. "Do you really believe she is in danger?"

He made no attempt to fob her off. "To be honest with you, ma'am, at this moment I'm not sure what I think. A week ago I would have said no, but . . ."

"You will have considered the obvious, of course—people like that steward his grace dismissed. I fear he did blame Perdita."

"It is a thought, certainly, but though I can well believe that he has been at the back of the earlier . . . pranks, for want of a better word, I don't somehow see him risking all by taking his grievance this far. But I shall know more when I have had words with the stable lad." St. Ive frowned. "What about that cousin of Perdita's?"

"Bertram Tillot? Oh, surely not!" Miss Midgely was clearly shaken by the suggestion. "He is spiteful enough, but I doubt he has the stomach for murder. Although . . ." Her eyes widened with sudden uncertainty.

"Yes?"

"It is not relevant, I am sure. He was drunk and in a raging temper at the time, just before he left us. But he *did* say—her voice trembled slightly over the words—"that he ought to have let the pediment fall on Perdita! Oh, but I'm sure he didn't mean it. Besides, the last we heard he was on . . ." She searched for the words. "On a winning streak. Is that what you call it? So he would have no motive, would he?"

"A gambler is always in need of money," said St. Ive dryly, and then, seeing the apprehension in her eyes, "I'm sorry, ma'am. I had not meant to worry you."

"No, no, my lord. I beg you will be open with me. I had far rather know how matters stand. I am exceedingly fond of Perdita—if it does not sound presumptuous, I would say that she is the nearest thing to family that I can lay claim to, so if there is ever anything you think I should know, I beg you will not hesitate to confide in me."

St. Ive took her hand in both of his. "I will. Believe me. It eases my mind considerably to know that Perdita has you." He turned and ran lightly down the steps.

"My lord—"

He turned.

"About Bertram Tillot. Perdita did mention to me a few days ago that she had heard a rumor of his being seen in the vicinity of Bath recently. Nowhere near here—up beyond Lansdown, I believe it was. But knowing how lacking in substance such rumors are—usually they originate with the uncle of a friend of a friend—I had not given it much credence." She smiled. "The residents of

Bath are very much given to such silliness, as I am sure you have had cause to know!"

"Yes indeed. But thank you for telling me all the same."

The marquis drove home in thoughtful mood. He went straight to the cottage belonging to his father's head groom, Jarvis, who had taken Jem in charge and had promised to keep him safe. Ample time had elasped for the lad to reflect upon his situation, and lest he forget, the bullet wound in his leg was a constant throbbing reminder. So that by the time the marquis arrived on the scene his bravado was in a fair way to crumbling. It took but a few well-chosen words on his lordship's part to effect his capitulation. The whole sorry tale came tumbling out.

St. Ive told the gist of this to his father later—how Jem had been coerced by the ex-steward into trying to frighten Perdita.

"The silly lad had been poaching a few rabbits on the side, and Benthall caught him at it and threatened him with dismissal if he didn't do as he was bade."

"So we were right in our suspicions about that fellow!" said the duke grimly. "I was too lenient with him before—but he'll know the full weight of the law this time, by God!" When his son was slow to agree, he looked more closely at him. "Well, out with it, my boy—what maggot is eating your brain now?"

St. Ive's face was expressionless. "I'm not sure. A maggot perhaps, but this particular maggot may turn out to be a poisonous little snake!"

"Dammit, Piers—be plain with me, if you please. I cannot abide riddles!"

The marquis shook his head as though coming out of a reverie. "I'm sorry to be tiresome, Father, but I have a niggling doubt at the back of my mind that what began as an act of spite on your ex-steward's part took a new turn today. The boy insisted that Benthall seemed edgy when he told him what he wanted done, as though . . ."

"As though someone was behind him, pushing?" suggested his grace with uncanny prescience. "Tillot, for example?"

"So you think it, too." St. Ive grinned. "Thank you. I had begun to wonder if I was becoming unhinged. There is absolutely nothing to connect Tillot and Benthall—yet I have this uneasy feeling that he is at the back of it somewhere."

His father looked at him. "So what will you do?"

"Make a few discreet inquiries locally, and then, if necessary, go to London."

"Perdita won't thank you for leaving her. Shall you tell her why?"

The marquis picked up his hat and gloves and strolled to the door. "I think not. It could all be a complete wild goose chase." At the door he paused and glanced back. "However, I would be obliged if you would do nothing about Benthall for the present. Apart from anything else, if he thinks he has got away with it, he'll be that much more confident—overconfident, maybe."

THE NEWS OF Perdita's betrothal to the marquis, though not yet officially announced, ran through Bath like a fire. Once Mrs. Windlesham knew of it—and there was no way of keeping it from her—the rest was inevitable.

"Why, you sly-puss!" she exclaimed with delight, having puffed up the stairs to see her young friend. "And here we were all thinking that Lord St. Ive was smitten with Lady Arabella Winton! Not but what I am not delighted, for it is no more than you deserve—and Lady Arabella for all her beauty and fine airs cannot hold a candle to you, besides which she is in no position to . . ." Here, to Perdita's amusement, Mrs. Windlesham's voice trailed away in embarrassment. She leaned forward to select a sugared plum from the dish of comfits her young friend was holding out to her before saying brightly and with quite a pointed change of direction, "You know, my dear, at one time I did wonder if you might not be tempted to settle for Mr. Gilles—for there was no doubt in my mind that he was dangling after you. I cannot tell you how relieved I am to know it is not so! And now I hear he is already paying court to a Miss Gooringe over Chippenham way—or was it Chichester? Anyhow, he has been offered a very superior living there by her father's contrivance and is to leave here very soon."

Perdita had heard. The clergyman had not been near them since his abortive proposal—and try as she might she could not be sorry. But for all that, she wished him happy in his latest conquest—an appointment to a town or city living would be much more to his taste—and she had little doubt of his becoming a dean or a canon before too long, which would puff him up no end.

Her own happiness was so great that she wished all the world well—even Miss Prothero. By being confined to the house for some time, she had been spared that good lady's probings into her affairs, but word came back to her that she was making a great deal of it—and was not beyond venturing a note of censure wherever she thought she might be sure of a sympathetic ear in consideration of how short a time had elapsed since the death of Sir Edwin.

All this Perdita took in good part. Nothing could dim her happiness—nothing, that is, except the absence of St. Ive for however short a time.

"Believe me, dearest, I shall not be away for one

moment longer than is necessary," he promised when she viewed his imminent desertion with mock reproach.

"So I should hope! Though if your mysterious business is, as I suspect, to bid a fond farewell to all your light o' loves, then I am not prepared to endure the separation with anything but reluctant stoicism! And I give you fair warning, from now on I do not mean to share you with anyone!"

"And I do not mean to wait for a lot of frippery nonsense before we can be married," he returned swiftly. "I shall obtain a special licence and you can buy all your bride clothes and gewgaws later!"

"Now that is a great deal too bad, sir," Perdita declared indignantly. "Do you mean to tell me that I have waited six and twenty years to be palmed off now with a hole-and-corner affair? For shame!" But the laughter in her eyes betrayed her, and soon she was begging for mercy and admitting that she would marry him on the morrow, in her shift if necessary.

Her knee healed rather more quickly than she could have hoped for, and soon she was able to drive into Bath without too much discomfort. Harry and Amaryllis returned from their visit to the country and were astonished to hear the glad news.

"I could not be more pleased," Amaryllis said warmly. "You deserve the very best—and Lord St. Ive will make the most attentive of husbands, I am sure, for he was always kindness itself to me." She blushed. "Oh dear. I did not mean . . . that is . . ."

Perdita laughed. "My dear, don't, pray, get yourself in a quake! I know exactly what you mean, and I don't blame him in the least for having been in love with you. My only wonder is my own good fortune that he should look twice at me having once desired you!"

Harry was more interested in her latest accident.

The story that was put about, that Perdita had slipped and twisted her knee, did not entirely convince him, and she caught him giving her a rather quizzical look. "It ain't like you to be so careless, old thing—first one thing, then another. Deuced smoky, if you ask me! Time someone took you in hand!"

They were at an evening party given by Mrs. Windlesham. She had expressed great regret when Perdita had arrived alone, without even the company of Miss Midgely, who was suffering from a slight indisposition.

"I had hoped, my dear, that I might be permitted to announce your engagement to Lord St. Ive, but there it is. Do you hope to have him back with you shortly?"

"I have no idea, ma'am, but I don't expect him to make a long stay in London." Perdita, resigned to the inevitability of some kind of celebration, smiled. "When he does return, I daresay we shall have to make a formal announcement—and give a party of our own."

It was not without relief that she was presently able to excuse herself and return home. The summer night was soft and mild—a new moon riding a sky crystal-clear and still faintly blue with here and there a star appearing. She was pleased to be alone—to indulge her foolish romantical fantasies in isolation.

Some time elasped, therefore, before she became aware that the road they were traveling, ill lit thought it was, was not familiar to her. It seemed a little strange that Silas should be taking a different route, but the thought did not trouble her unduly until the coach stopped. By now it was very much darker, but not so dark as to prevent her from seeing that the house before which they had come to a halt was not Marston Grange, but something much smaller and meaner.

Before she had time to call out, the door had opened and the figure of her cousin Bertram stood revealed in the dim light of the coach lamps.

"Bertie!" she exclaimed, more angry than alarmed. "What is the meaning of this? Where is this place?"

"All in good time, dear coz," said Bertram Tillot. "Be so kind as to step down and we can discuss the matter indoors."

Chapter 17

*I*T WAS MIDMORNING when St. Ive arrived back from London. The doors of Anderley Court swung open to receive him as he ran up the steps, shrugging off his voluminous driving coat and handing it with his hat and gauntlets to Pendlebury.

"My father about yet?" he enquired tersely.

"In the library, my lord," murmured the butler, passing the garments to a waiting footman. Something in his tone made the marquis shoot him a look that was decidedly inquisitorial. Pendlebury cleared his throat. "His grace has Miss Midgely with him, my lord, and I fear they are both somewhat disturbed."

St. Ive's features assumed an even more forbidding aspect, strangely reminiscent of the old duke. Without a word he strode across the hall and flung open the library door without ceremony. The tension in the atmosphere was immediately discernible, and the two pairs of eyes that turned to him confirmed that the news was bad.

"Piers—thank God you are come!"

His father, usually so decisive, sounded for once ragged with worry, and without waiting to be told, he knew. "Perdita," he snapped. "Something has happened to her!"

Miss Midgely, her nose tinged with pink, her eyes red-rimmed, sat rigidly erect, facing his father. It was as though only the discipline of years was holding her in check.

"Perdita," she said in a clear, carefully controlled voice, "went alone last evening to a small party given by Mrs. Windlesham. I was suffering from a heavy cold and did not accompany her. When Fletcher came to inform me that she had not returned, I am ashamed to say that I assumed that, the weather having turned most inclement, she had determined to stay the night." Miss Midgely twisted a handkerchief convulsively between nervous fingers. "It was not until this morning, when our coachman returned with a broken head and some garbled tale of having been set upon, that I realized what an appalling mistake I had made."

"My dear ma'am," the duke interposed, "you really must not hold yourself to blame."

"But I am to blame. I should have known that Perdita would not follow such a course of action without letting me know. If I had been feeling more myself . . ."

Sympathetic as St. Ive was to Miss Midgely's distress, he lacked the patience to reassure her. "Nothing is to be gained by dwelling upon might-have-beens," he said. "The thing is, where is Perdita now?"

The duke held out a sheet of paper. "This came about two hours ago. I sent for Miss Midgely at once."

St. Ive strode across to his father's chair beside the fire and all but snatched the missive from his fingers.

"It is, as you see, unsigned," commented the duke tautly as his son swiftly scanned the page.

The message, addressed jointly to the duke and his son, stated that Miss Grant was being held prisoner, and would be returned only upon the payment of a sum of fifty thousand pounds—a sum well within the scope of both gentlemen—the money to be deposited at a given venue within twenty-four hours. Any attempt to deviate from the instructions or to attempt to discover Miss Grant's whereabouts would result in her instant demise.

For a long moment St. Ive couldn't trust himself to speak. When he at last did so his voice grated on the air. "Tillot. It has to be Tillot, probably aided by that Benthall man. He could never accomplish the thing alone."

"That was my first thought," His father agreed. "Did anything you found out in London give you reason for such confidence?"

The marquis heard the faint echo of his own anguish in his father's voice. "I believe so. Enough, in fact, to make it almost a certainty. Tillot is head over ears in debt—more so than ever before."

"But . . ." Miss Midgely was bemused. "Harry— Sir Henry Munro, that is—told Perdita that Bertram's fortunes had undergone a complete reversal and that he was now quite wealthy."

St. Ive's mouth twisted. "With men like Tillot, such luck is seldom sustained, for they never learn from experience. His case ran true to form." He strode to the door and shouted for Pendlebury. "Send word to the stables. I want fresh horses put to at once! And bring me my hat and coat."

"About the money, Piers—" Anderley began.

"Forget it. Tillot isn't getting one penny if I have anything to say to it!" He was almost out of the room when Miss Midgely cried out to him, and he turned back impatiently.

"Forgive me, my lord, but if you do not mean to pay the ransom, what do you intend to do?"

There was a glittering light in his eyes as he

replied, "Do, ma'am? I am going to get Perdita back." And he was gone.

She turned apprehensively to the duke. "Sir, I have no wish to appear to question Lord St. Ive's wisdom in this. Indeed, his confidence does inspire one to hope. But if he should not succeed . . . the threat contained in that awful letter . . ." Miss Midgely was ashamed to find herself succumbing to tears.

The duke rose and crossed slowly to her side, resting his hand comfortingly on her shoulder. "My dear ma'am, pray do not distress yourself. Piers found out quite a number of interesting facts about Tillot even before he went to London, and about several friends he made in the Lansdown area while he was staying here. It is one of these so-called friends in whose employ Benthall now is. Piers must believe that there is a connection to be made—and I . . ." The duke hesitated before concluding firmly, "I have every confidence in my son's ability to know what he is about, and to succeed in his bid to bring Perdita safe home."

PERDITA WAS AT THAT very moment rousing from a drugged sleep, cramped, confused, and with a head that throbbed abominably. As she attempted to ease herself into a more comfortable position, the cause of her discomfort became apparent. She was lying on a rough wooden settle, and her hands and feet were bound fast, while an attempt to lift her head sent stabbing pains shooting from her neck and shoulders up into her very skull.

In growing dismay she sank back, and recollection came flooding in. Oh, how could she have been so easily taken in? So lost in foolish contemplation of love that she had paid such scant heed to the direction taken by the carriage! It wasn't until it stopped and she saw her cousin standing there at the open door of what appeared to be a tiny, insignificant dwelling that the full extent of her stupidity dawned upon her. Her first thought was of flight, but when she saw the man whom she recognized instantly as the duke's ex-steward climbing down from the box, she knew that any attempt at escape would be both pointless and undignified. With an outward appearance of calm, she stepped past Bertram and into the cottage, though inwardly she was shaking with rage and apprehension.

As he shut the door she turned to face him, mustering all the authority she could command. "Bertram, what the devil is the meaning of this nonsense?"

"No nonsense, dear coz, I assure you. I am in deadly earnest!"

The room they were in was but dimly lit—enough, however, to see that it was sparsely furnished and had few of the modest comforts to be found in similar dwellings in Anderley. Against such a background Bertram's dandified appearance seemed incongruous to say the least, and yet something in his confident manner offset that incongruity and created an air of menace.

"I suppose I may imagine what your accomplice has done with Silas."

"Your coachman?" Bertram shrugged. "A tap on the head, I daresay. Enough to give him a sore head for a few days."

"Your behavior is despicable, and its purpose quite beyond my comprehension," she said coldly. "If it is some kind of joke, then you have badly missed your mark, let me tell you, so you had as well take me home at once."

She had spoken without any real hope of being heeded, but what she had not expected was that he would find her demand amusing, or that in his

smile there would be a strange excitement that
was distinctly unnerving. He stepped closer and
pushed her none too gently toward the settle until
she had no alternative but to sit.

"You aren't going anywhere, coz. It might interest you to know that you are about to become a
valuable property."

A creeping fear lent urgency to her exasperation. "Oh, really, Bertie! For heaven's sake do talk
sense! We have already been through all this. If
you imagine you are going to get one penny more
out of me by keeping me here, you are quite out.
Such stupidity will only serve to strengthen my
resolve!"

She was a little disconcerted to find that her
words caused him even more amusement.

"I don't want money from you, Perdita. After all,
why settle for milk when with a little ingenuity
you can have all the cream you want?" He enjoyed
the look of mystification on her face to the full
before concluding, "I have devised a much more
profitable scheme—brilliant, in fact. You see, my
dear coz, I have decided to ransom you!"

"Ransom?" Perdita attempted to rise, but he was
standing too close to her. She had to crane her
neck back to look up into his face, which had
grown smug. "Is your brain completely addled?"
she exclaimed. "I never heard anything so nonsensical in my life!"

This wiped the smug look off his face, but the
rancor that replaced it was if anything more worrying. "We'll see how nonsensical it is when your
precious duke and his son get my demand for your
safe return. The alternative I presented them with
will leave them little choice but to pay if they ever
hope to see you again!"

For once Perdita was robbed of speech. Before
she could recover her wits, the man Benthall had

come back into the room. He glowered and jerked his head in her direction.

"Well, that's the carriage stowed. What d'you mean to do with her? Give her free rein, by God, and she'll be away, mark my words!" He came closer, and Perdita could see the bitterness in his eyes. "Just say the word and I'll give her what I gave her coachman. It's no more than the bitch deserves!"

The smug look had returned to Bertram's face. "Maybe, but we've had enough of your bungling." He watched with a certain pleasure the ugly red tide of color that disfigured the man's face. "Besides, there is more than one way to deal with recalcitrant people like my cousin Perdita." He withdrew a small flask from his pocket. "If you would be so good as to restrain her for just a moment, I will show you how simple it can be."

Benthall seized her arms from behind, pinning her against the hard back of the settle and using far more force than was necessary out of sheer pleasure, or so it seemed to Perdita. In spite of a very real fear she kept her mouth resolutely closed as Bertram rammed the flask hard against her lips until, by the simple expediency of pinching her nostrils together, he obliged her to open them for air. Quick as a flash, he tipped the bitter liquid into her mouth, and most of it found its way irresistibly down her throat. Laudanum, she thought woozily as it began to take effect. It was her last coherent thought—that and the memory of Bertram's face leering very close to her own, and his gleeful voice murmuring, "Have a good long sleep, coz!"

And sleep she had until this moment, when a persistent high-pitched noise awoke her. Her eyelids felt heavy, but the oddest sensation that she was being watched presently obliged her to open them to the hurtful light. Two small children were standing regarding her with solemn incurious eyes, the younger no more than two years old with his thumb stuck comfortingly in his mouth; the other, looking little older, had both hands pushed into the pockets of a loose-woven smock. The noise, which was growing louder by the minute, proved to be that of a baby screaming somewhere beyond her range of vision.

Perdita tried to speak, but found her mouth parched and bitter-tasting. "A drink," she managed at last, but to little effect. The children continued to stare unblinking.

From somewhere nearby a plaintive voice wearily besought Benny to mind his sister. The elder of the two boys trotted away obediently, and a moment later the thudding and squeaking of a cradle being rocked added to the undiminishing clamor.

"Oh, Fanny, be quiet, do!" The voice grew shrill. "I've only got one pair of hands!"

Sheer curiosity gripped Perdita, tempting her to master the numbing cramp that pervaded her limbs. Supporting herself on one elbow, she edged her legs around until her feet were touching the uneven flags of the floor, then she levered herself upright. At this point a nauseating dizziness threatened to overwhelm her. She closed her eyes and sat very still until the pounding in her head eased and she was able to open them again.

By day the room looked even shabbier than it had in the lamplight of the previous evening, and pathetically inadequate for a family's use. Apart from the settle she occupied, the only furniture seemed to consist of a small scrubbed table and two stools near the window, a cupboard set against the rough masonry wall, and a deep stone sink where a too-thin young woman stood struggling with a mountain of washing. On the other side of the room was a low opening scarcely big enough to hold a bed.

"Do you think I might have a drink?" she croaked a little louder as the baby paused to draw breath.

The woman turned, dull-eyed. "Oh, so you're awake, are you?" With a shrug she dried her hands on a cloth and poured some water from a jug into a tin mug. She brought it across and held it to Perdita's lips. Perdita gulped greedily, spluttering over the brackish water. But at least it eased her parched throat.

"I suppose you wouldn't consider untying my hands?"

"No, she wouldn't. Not if she values her hide." Benthall had entered unheard above the clamor of the baby's crying. "Can't you shut that brat up, Ellen?"

"She's hungry," the woman muttered listlessly. "What d'you expect? I haven't got anywhere near enough milk to satisfy her."

"Well, give her a spoonful of gin, for God's sake! Anything to stop that din!" Benthall turned back to Perdita. "So what's it like to come slumming, eh?"

"I've seen worse, but not much," she said tersely.

"Ah, but it's one thing playing Lady Bountiful, and quite another having to live in such a hovel! I mean, it's not exactly Anderley Court, is it? Or even Marston Grange!"

She ignored the taunt. "Where is my cousin?"

He uttered a derisive snort of laughter. "Still in his bed, belike—or primping himself and deciding what he'll do with all the money you're about to make for him! Our Mr. Tillot don't care to concern himself with the more sordid details of kidnap. Leaves that to the likes of me."

"Well, I hope he's paying you well," Perdita said, judging that there was something less than harmony between the two men. "And I hope you get

the money. My cousin is not always scrupulous
where money is concerned, and I guess he will be
picking up the ransom himself."

Benthall's face took on an ugly travesty of a
smile. "Very clever, Miss Highty-tighty! Trying to
set us against one another won't wash, and if you
thought it would, you don't know Fred Benthall!
Because if matters *did* fall out that way, your painted
tulip of a cousin would very quickly learn that it
don't do to cross me, and so you may tell him if
you see him."

His face had been pushed close into hers, but
now he straightened up. "I've got to go now. Ellen,
don't you fall for this one's glib tongue. I wouldn't
be surprised if she hadn't got more tricks up her
sleeve than a monkey! And if I find you've been
letting her loose, you'll regret it."

"But I got to feed her," said the woman. "Though
God knows what with!"

Benthall walked to the door. "Let her be. It won't
do her any harm to starve a little—show her what
it's like to go without."

When he had gone, time began to drag. Perdita's
headache had subsided to a dull ache, and she
occupied herself in watching the young woman
going about her work. The mountain of washing
never seemed to grow less, and there was always a
pot of water heating on the fire in the small grate.

"I take it in from the houses round about," she
told Perdita as she stopped for a few moments to
cut a thick wad of bread for each of the two boys,
complete with a scrape of dripping. "It brings in a
few pence extra, and with my man away . . ."

"Where is he?"

"He's been sent north to one of Sir James's other
houses—beating for the grouse shoot, but it don't
mean extra money, and no one thinks how we're
supposed to live in the meantime."

"Is that why you're doing this?" Perdita asked. "To make a little extra? I suppose Benthall must be paying you something to keep me hidden."

"Not him." Ellen shrugged, her voice bitter. She picked up the baby, who was still grizzling, and walked across to one of the stools. She put the child to an inadequate breast, clearly an unfulfilling experience for both parties. "He simply threatened to have Jack dismissed if I didn't do as he wanted." A weak tear trickled down one cheek.

"But that's monstrous!"

"It's life, ma'am. For the likes of us, that is."

Perdita was filled with an impotent rage. The girl, for she was probably not even as old as herself, looked pinched and worn to a thread—any prettiness she might once have possessed ground out of her by poverty and hopelessness.

"Will Benthall be back soon, do you think?"

Ellen shook her head. "He hasn't been here long enough to take liberties with Sir James. But it's no good you thinking I'll help you, because he'd know in the end. You're a decent lady, and I'm sorry for your plight, but I have myself and the little ones to think about. I *daren't* take the chance!"

Perdita weighed up her chances of making the woman change her mind, and felt that they were not great; and while she had every expectation that the duke had already initiated investigations, she had no desire to remain helplessly trussed up like a chicken waiting upon her cousin's pleasure should he choose to turn really nasty. If she were honest, her most fervent hope was that St. Ive would have returned from London and by some omniscient power generated by their love would discover her whereabouts and arrive to rescue her before her situation became desperate. However, being of a practical disposition, she felt that to be relying upon near-miracles of chance without making a push to help herself would be unrealistic, not to say downright foolhardy.

Ellen had laid the baby back in the cradle without, Perdita noticed both from the smell and the look of her, relieving her of her wet and uncomfortable garments, so that poor little Fanny, unsatisfied on all counts, was not slow to make her misery felt.

It was, for Ellen, the last straw. The tears, so close for so long, came flooding out. She sank onto the settle beside Perdita, gulping between sobs, "If only I w-wasn't so tired! S-sometimes I wish I was dead!"

Perdita, feeling her helplessness even more and deeply moved by the girl's plight, forced herself to speak in calm quiet tones. "Look—I know how frightened you are, but if you will only untie these ridiculous ropes, I give you my solemn word that I won't attempt to leave, nor will I permit anyone to harm you."

Ellen, surprised in midsob, lifted her head slowly and stared at her as though she were demented. "That's daft." She gulped. "Why would you stay here when you could get clean away?"

Perdita smiled wryly. "I suppose it does verge on the unbelievable. But you see, I do most strongly object to being used this way, and I have no intention of leaving without crushing my cousin's pretentions, once and for all! Believe me, I do know what I'm about." Her smile broadened. "My dear Ellen—I may call you Ellen, may I not?" The girl nodded in a bemused way. "I promise you that I'm not 'dicked in the nob'! But it doesn't require any great powers of observation to see how exhausted you are. If you will release me, I will engage to look after your children while you take a much-needed rest. So what do you say?"

The suggestion appeared to have deprived the

girl of speech entirely. She took a little convincing, but the thought of sleep soon overcame all other considerations, and she agreed. By the time Perdita was free and had rubbed some life back into her hands and feet, Ellen was already curled up in the corner bed and fast asleep.

It was only then that Perdita realized what she had promised, and realized too that she hadn't the first idea how to go about it. She looked around the shabby room—at the pile of washing, completed and ready to be dried and at the even bigger pile still waiting to be done. The children were still in awe of her and the baby was still crying.

"Oh, well!" She shrugged, half humorously, and turned to survey the waiting pile of washing. "Benny, will you show me where your mama usually dries these?"

Wordlessly he took Perdita by the hand and led her to a back door. Beyond it there was a small stretch of overgrown grass, above which was strung a washing line. The rain of the previous evening had left the ground saturated, so that her feet were soon in a similar state, but the sun was shining and with any luck the strong breeze would soon dry the linen, which, with Benny's help, she soon had blowing from the line. Indoors, she surveyed the unwashed pile and decided that charity could only extend so far, and that the children must be her first priority.

She investigated the cupboards and found the contents woefully inadequate. What she did discover, however, tucked away at the back of one of them, was a shotgun—unloaded, she guessed, but it still might serve her in case of necessity. She left it where it might easily be reached.

The next hour or so passed quickly. Perdita had never worked so hard in her life, but, never one to resist a challenge, she enjoyed herself more than she would have believed possible. She changed the baby and amused the two little boys, and as Benny became more forthcoming, she learned that his brother was called Jason, a misnomer if ever she'd heard one. He continued to suck his thumb and followed her everywhere like a shadow.

The time came when she was sure they must be hungry, but what to give them? She remembered the hens she had seen scratching around in the hedgerow around the back of the cottage. "Are they yours?" she asked Benny without any hope of being answered, but to her surprise he ventured into speech, muttering that they belonged to the home farm.

"Well, if they have laid any eggs, I don't think the home farm will miss a few," she said firmly, and they spent the next few minutes searching the undergrowth to emerge triumphant bearing six brown eggs, still warm. It was then a matter of finding a suitable pan to boil them in, filling it with water from the pot on the fire, and having built up the fire, setting it to boil with four of the eggs in it, reserving the other two for Ellen when she awoke. At this point Perdita discovered that she had no idea how long it would take to boil them, but guessed that it could not be much above a minute or two.

By the time she had lifted them out and cut some of the remaining bread, the baby was crying again. Quickly she found a couple of plates and spooned two of the eggs into them, motioning the boys to the table and settling them with spoons and the bread, before picking the child up. Her chief worry, that the screaming would wake Ellen, proved unfounded, for she slept as one dead.

With the baby's cries so close to her ear, Perdita almost missed the sound of the door latch lifting.

Without turning around she eased her way toward the cupaboard and felt for the shotgun.

"Good God!" drawled a blessedly familiar voice, and she swung around to see St. Ive in the doorway, immaculate as ever, his eyeglass raised to view the extraordinary scene.

She ran to him and was crushed to his breast, shotgun and baby and all, while she confessed incoherently how much she had wished for him to come and how difficult everything was, and finally asked how he came to be there at all.

"I came to rescue you," he admitted drolly. "But it seems that you are managing very well without me." He extracted the shotgun, which was pressed somewhat precariously against his heart, and laid it carefully on the table.

"Oh, it's all right," Perdita said. "It isn't loaded—at least, I don't think it is. I haven't actually had time to check, what with the washing and feeding the children . . ." She stopped as she saw that the boys had cleaned their plates and waited, spoons poised expectantly, watching with interest.

"Oh! Dearest St. Ive, do hold Fanny for a moment while I . . ." She quickly brought the other two eggs and spooned them out onto the boys' plates. "There is very little bread left, I'm afraid," she said. "Can you manage without, do you think?"

They proceeded to demonstrate how well, and she left them to it, giving all her attention to St. Ive once more. He was holding the baby very gingerly, and the look of acute distaste on his handsome features gave some clue as to the cause. The incongruity of the situation suddenly hit her, and she began to laugh, sheer relief adding impetus to her mirth.

"Perdita," he said in deceptively gentle tones. "Will you be so good as to remove this . . . child, which appears to be in urgent need of attention, I may say, and tell me what the devil is going on? I come here, driven almost to desperation, and expecting to find you in the direst peril, and instead you appear to be playing housekeeper to a pack of brats."

"Hush, my lord, you will hurt their feelings," she murmured, taking the baby from him and popping her back into the cradle, where she continued to bawl lustily. St. Ive's mouth tightened ominously.

"Their feelings be damned! At this moment I am more concerned with mine! I warn you, if this is some kind of joke—"

"No, indeed!" Perdita held out her hands to him, all desire to laugh leaving her. He jerked her forward, crushing her. "If I seem to be taking all this lightly," she said into his coat, "it is because I am feeling light-headed with the sheer joy and relief of having you here! And truly, I have been—still am, I suppose—in the direst peril!"

She explained to him all that had happened, held safe in the comfort of his arms. "Are you telling me," he demanded when she had finished, "that you had the chance to escape and didn't take it?"

"Well, but how could I? I had given this poor woman my word, and would not for the world walk out on her!"

"Oh, Perdita!" His mouth found hers, devouring her as though he would never let her go. When finally he lifted his head, his voice had grown a little unsteady. "No one but you would do anything so—quixotic! Did it never cross your mind that Tillot might come? Or worse still, that creature Benthall?"

"Well, of course it did. In fact, I very much hoped that Bertram would come," she said. "I have a great deal to say to him! I'll allow that I feel less confident about Benthall, though when I consider how he has frightened this poor woman, I believe I might even give a fair account of myself with him!"

It was St. Ive's turn to laugh. "My love, you are incorrigible! However, you will be spared that at least. Benthall has been dealt with."

Perdita leaned back within his arms to look up at him. "He has?"

"I met Harry Munro in Bath, and when I told him what had happened, nothing would do but that he should come with me. We intercepted Benthall on his way here, and . . . took care of him."

"Killed him, do you mean? Oh, my lord!" She stepped back, and he allowed her to do so, sliding his hands down her arms until he held her only by the wrists.

"Not quite." His voice sounded almost savage. "But he is trussed up ready for the magistrate to deal with. We have put him safely out of sight for the present. Until your cousin too has been dealt with."

Perdita looked up into his face, uncompromising in its stark lines. "You won't . . . that is, does he have to be handed over to the magistrates as well?"

"Perdita! After all that has happened?"

She moved uneasily. "Yes, I know. He is not worthy of my consideration, even of my pity. Yet I still feel a kind of responsibility, and no matter how idiotish you think me . . ."

He drew her forward and kissed her gently. "One day I will tell you exactly what I think of you. For the present, I want you to go with Harry and leave me to deal with Bertram. We found your carriage hidden in a kind of shed."

As if on cue, Harry put his head in the door. "Everything all right, is it?" He grinned a little sheepishly. "You've given us all a devil of a worrying time, love."

"Oh dear, poor Midge! And his grace!" She looked at St. Ive. "Were they very distressed?"

"You could say that," he murmured dryly. "But your safe return will soon put an end to that." He turned to Harry. "Will you be so good as to take Perdita home now while I wait for Tillot?"

"But I can't just go and leave poor Ellen here!" Perdita objected. "I promised I would not, and she will think I have let her down!"

St. Ive sighed in exasperation. "Then you will have to wake her and explain. But be quick about it, my love, I beg of you!"

"And money," she said. "I must leave her some money. She has been so kind, and she is quite destitute, you know."

It seemed an unconscionable time to St. Ive while she shook Ellen awake, told her what was happening, reassured her, and kissed all the children. He exchanged a wry glance with Harry, who shrugged and said that that was Perdita for you. St. Ive produced half a dozen sovereigns, which the woman eyed with disbelief but was persuaded to take, and finally chivvied Perdita out of the house.

"You will be careful?" were her parting words. "I still think I should stay."

"Harry," besought St. Ive. "Take her away, there's a good fellow!"

Chapter 18

*I*T WAS SOME LITTLE TIME before Bertram Tillot
arrived—time during which an air of unease prevailed, Ellen being totally overawed by the presence of so august a personage in her parlor,
lounging upon the settle and filling the room with
the force of his personality.

It came as a relief to both parties, therefore,
when the door latch clicked at last and the dandified figure of Bertram Tillot stood revealed in the
opening. St. Ive rose unhurriedly and turned to
face him.

The look of blank horror in Bertram's eyes gave
way almost immediately to panic and fear. He turned
to run.

"Don't," the marquis advised silkily. "I should be
obliged to shoot you, and while I might think the
world would be a better place without you, I would
as lief dispose of you in a less messy fashion. Come
in and shut the door."

"Where is Perdita?" Bertram's voice was little
more than a croak.

"By now, at home, I should think. I fear your
pathetic attempt to ransom her has gone badly
amiss."

"You devil! Is there nothing you don't know?"

"Very little, I imagine." The marquis turned to Ellen. "I wonder, ma'am, would you be so good as to take the children into the garden? The weather is not unpleasant, and there are things to be said and done here which are better said and done in private."

Ellen bobbed a curtsy and rushed to pick up the baby. "Yes, m'lord. I've the washing to see to. Come, Benny, Jason. P'raps your lordship'll be so good as to let me know when you've done."

In the silence that followed their departure, St. Ive could almost sense the other man's fear as a tangible thing. "I find that I have come to the end of my patience with you, Tillot," he began. "It was bad enough when you attempted to saddle Miss Grant with your debts, but far from being grateful for being saved from your stupidity, you have devised this latest piece of wickedness in which you have not only had the impertinence to cause your cousin to be molested and frightened on several occasions, but also distressed my father out of sheer greed. These things I cannot forgive."

Bertram muttered, red-faced, that it was all very well for those with unlimited funds to preach at those less fortunate, but St. Ive cut in on him ruthlessly.

"You have had money enough, and it has run through your fingers like water. And now you have turned to crime, which has resulted in equally dismal failure. Your accomplice is already in the hands of the law, and if he runs true to form, he will even now be singing his head off to implicate you, so you will soon be joining him."

"You can't do that!" Bertram's voice had grown shrill. "Perdita won't let you! Blood is still thicker than water!"

"Not in this case," St. Ive said softly, standing

close and looking at him in a way that had reduced stronger men than Bertram to a quivering wreck. "Not after what you have tried to do this day."

"Even so," he stammered, "she won't have me put in prison!"

"Perdita will not have the power to prevent it. If nothing else, I can have you committed for debt."

"You?" Bertrand stared. "But I don't owe you—"

"Oh, but you do, Tillot. In fact, you owe me a considerable amount. You see, while I was in London recently, I took the opportunity to buy up all your debts, so I am now your sole creditor—and if you do not do exactly as I say, you will languish in prison for as long as it pleases me to have you do so."

Bertram slumped, all the fight suddenly knocked out of him.

"However," St. Ive continued, "there is another choice open to you, and if you will do exactly as I say, you may yet save your miserable hide."

PERDITA WAITED AT Anderley Court for most of that evening, but St. Ive did not come. The thought that something must have happened to him stayed with her through a sleepless night though she made light of his continuing absence in the duke's company, for he did look quite worn.

"He did say he might be quite some time," she said reassuringly as she left him on that first evening, "so you must not worry if he does not come. My cousin is incapable of doing anyone harm, least of all someone like Piers, without some bullyboy to aid him, and Benthall is safely locked away by now."

But all her fine words did not help her to conquer her own fears that Bertram might have had other accomplices. At breakfast the following morning, Miss Midgely looked at her with some concern.

"Have you closed your eyes at all?" she asked bluntly, and when Perdita prevaricated, "I do think you might have faith in Lord St. Ive's ability to look after himself."

"Well, of course I do!" Perdita exclaimed. "I simply wish to have him back."

But she was at Anderley Court almost before the duke was awake, let alone up and about. She went to sit in the garden room, but for once it had lost its power to soothe her. She stared down into the pool, where even the fish seemed sluggish in the early sunlight, and heard nothing, was aware of nothing until a shadow that had not been there a moment before appeared on the water next to her own.

Arms closed round her, and with a skirl of joy she turned to be crushed in St. Ive's embrace and ruthlessly kissed.

"Oh, how could you?" she cried, when she could draw breath. "To creep up on me in that way when I have been imagining you lying dead or mortally injured!"

"What?" He laughed down at her. "At your cousin's hands? I am grossly insulted, my dearest girl, that you should think it even for a moment!"

It was some time before they came around to any coherent explanations. But sooner or later it was inevitable that Perdita should wish to know what had happened.

"Your cousin, my love, is by now on his way to France," said St. Ive with what she considered odious complacency. "And if he ever shows his face here again, I will have him in prison so fast his feet won't touch the ground."

"You're quite sure he has gone?" Perdita urged. "We have thought him vanquished more than once."

St. Ive looked down at her reproachfully. "You thought him vaniquished. If you remember, I had my doubts, even then. This time, I have put him on the boat myself, and since I hold all his debts, he is in no position to return." His expression was for a moment forbidding. "If he should ever be tempted, he knows that I shall kill him."

Perdita drew away a little. "But you wouldn't? I can't believe . . ."

He pulled her back. "The important thing to remember, my dearest girl, is that he *does* believe it. Now, if you have no objection, I should very much like to consign your cousin and all his nasty little ways to perdition." His mouth was very close to hers. "I have much better things to do with my time."

About the Author

SHEILA WALSH LIVES with her husband in Southport, Lancashire, England, and is the mother of two daughters. She began to think seriously about writing when a local writers' club was formed. After experimenting with short stories and plays, she completed her first Regency novel, THE GOLDEN SONGBIRD, which subsequently won her an award presented by the Romantic Novelists' Association in 1974.

Introducing a new
historical romance by Joan Wolf

DESIRE'S INSISTENT SONG CARRIED THEIR PASSION THROUGH THE FLAMES OF LOVE AND WAR . . .

The handsome Virginian made Lady Barbara Carr shiver with fear and desire. He was her new husband, a stranger, wed to her so his wealth could pay her father's debts, an American patriot, sworn to fight Britain's king. But Alan Maxwell had never wanted any woman the way he wanted this delicate English lady. And a hot need ignited within him as he carried Barbara to the canopied bed, defying the danger of making her his bride tonight . . . when war could make her his enemy tomorrow. . . .

Coming in July from Signet!

The sensuous adventure that began with

SKYE O'MALLEY

continues in . . .

He is Skye O'Malley's younger brother, the handsomest rogue in Queen Elizabeth's court . . . She is a beautiful stranger . . . When Conn O'Malley's roving eye beholds Aidan St. Michael, they plunge into an erotic adventure of unquenchable desire and exquisite passion that binds them body and soul in a true union of the heart. But when a cruel betrayal makes Conn a prisoner in the Tower, and his cherished Aidan a harem slave to a rapacious sultan, Aidan must use all her skill in ecstasy's dark arts to free herself—and to be reunited forever with the only man she can ever love. . . .

**A breathtaking, hot-blooded saga
of tantalizing passion and ravishing desire**

Coming in July from Signet!